Class Warfare

NOAM CHOMSKY

Interviews with David Barsamian

Viva Books

New Delhi | Mumbai | Chennai | Kolkata | Bangalore | Hyderabad | Kochi

First Indian Edition 2008

VIVA BOOKS PRIVATE LIMITED

- 4737/23 Ansari Road, Daryaganj, New Delhi 110 002
  E-mail: vivadelhi@vivagroupindia.net, Tel. 42242200
- 76, Service Industries, Shirvane, Sector 1, Nerul, Navi Mumbai 400 706
  E-mail: vivamumbai@vivagroupindia.net, Tel. 27721273, 27721274
- Jamals Fazal Chambers, 26 Greams Road, Chennai 600 006
  E-mail: vivachennai@vivagroupindia.net, Tel. 28290304, 28294241
- B-103, Jindal Towers, 21/1A/3 Darga Road, Kolkata 700 017
  E-mail: vivakolkata@vivagroupindia.net, Tel. 22836381, 22816713
- 7, Sovereign Park Apartments, 56-58, K. R. Road, Basavanagudi, Bangalore 560 004
  E-mail: vivabangalore@vivagroupindia.net, Tel. 26607409, 26607410
- 101-102 Mughal Marc Apartments, 3-4-637 to 641, Narayanguda, Hyderabad 500 029
  E-mail: vivahyderabad@vivagroupindia.net, Tel. 27564481, 27564482
- First Floor, Beevi Towers, SRM Road, Kaloor, Kochi 682 018, Kerala
  E-mail: vivakochi@vivagroupindia.net, Tel: 0484-2403055, 2403056

Published by arrangement with

Pluto Press
345, Archway Road,
London N6 5AA

ISBN-10: 81-309-0625-2
ISBN-13: 978-81-309-0625-6

Published by Vinod Vasishtha for Viva Books Private Limited, 4737/23, Ansari Road, New Delhi 110 002. Printed and bound by Anand Sons, Delhi - 110 092.

Contents

Introduction

In this third book in a series of interview collections, Noam Chomsky begins with comments about the right-wing agenda that have turned out to be prescient. Corporations with their political allies are waging an unrelenting class war against working people. A vast social engineering project is being implemented under the guise of fiscal responsibility. In this latest incarnation of class warfare, there is no doubt as to which side Chomsky is on. For him, solidarity is not an abstract concept but a vital and unifying principle.

The interviews were recorded in Chomsky's office at MIT and by phone from 1994 to 1996. Some were broadcast nationally and internationally as part of my Alternative Radio weekly series. Others were aired on KGNU in Boulder, Colorado.

The accolades and accusations accorded Noam Chomsky are too numerous—and too well known—to warrant discussion here. For those sympathetic to his views there are a number of possible responses. One is to stand in awe of his prolific output and unwavering principles, limited by the sense that his abilities are unmatchable. A second choice is to implement his simple formula for learning about the world and creating social change: "There has not in history ever been any answer other than, Get to work on it." Indeed, it's not like mastering quantum physics or learning Sanskrit.

Class Warfare is provided in the hopes the reader might choose to engage in political action. After countless books, interviews, articles and speeches, Chomsky concludes with one wish: "What I should be doing is way more of this kind of thing." That a person of his commitment is seeking ways to increase his contribution is, for me, a source of continued inspiration.

—David Barsamian
March 10, 1996

Looking Ahead

Tenth Anniversary Interview

December 20, 1994

DB *Noam, it was ten years ago that we did our first interview. I know that you do so few interviews it probably is very vivid in your mind.*

Absolutely. I recall every word [laughs].

DB *I remember it well because I had all sorts of technical problems. I couldn't operate the tape recorder. I called you and said, We can't do it. Then I managed to figure it out. Anyway, that was ten years ago. A review of* Keeping the Rabble in Line *says we have a "symbiotic relationship." Is that something that we need to worry about?*

As long as it's symbiotic at long distance, I guess it's OK.

DB *All right, good. Actually, we usually end on this kind of note. I want to start with your upcoming plans. I know you have a trip to Australia coming up in January.*

That one's been in the works for about twenty years, I guess.

DB *Any new books?*

Right now I'm in the middle of a very technical book on linguistics and I have in the back of my mind a long-promised book on the philosophy of language. On the political issues, I'm not exactly sure. I might be putting together some essays and updating them. Several people have asked for updated and extended essays on current matters and I might do that. I'm not really sure. I have sort of a feeling that I've saturated the market a bit with books. I might wait a while.

DB *How about writing for Z? Are you going to continue that?*

Oh, sure. I have a couple of articles coming out right now. There's a long one, which was too long, so it was broken into two parts. It will be coming out in January and February. There's a bunch of other things. And other journals.

DB *The last time we had a conversation you said that the linguistics work was particularly exciting. There was a certain animation in your voice. What particularly is attractive to you about the work you're doing now in linguistics?*

It's hard to explain easily. There's a kind of a rhythm to any work, I think, probably to any scientific work. Some interesting ideas come along and change the way you look at things. A lot of people start trying them and applying them. They find all kinds of difficulties and try to work it out. There's a period of working on things within a relatively fixed framework. At some point they converge, or something leaps out at you and you suddenly see there's another way of looking at it that is much better than the old one and that will put to rest a lot of the problems that people have been grappling with. Now you go off to a new stage. Right now there's a good chance that it's that kind of moment, which for me at least has happened maybe two or three times before altogether. It happens to be particularly exciting this time. There seems to be a way possibly to show that a core part of human language, the core part of the mechanisms that relate sound and meaning, are not only largely universal, but in fact even from a certain point of view virtually optimal. Meaning on very general considerations if you were to design a system, like if you were God designing a system, you would come close to doing it this way. There are a lot of remarkable things about language anyway. It has properties that, it has been known for a long time, you just wouldn't expect a biological organism to have at all, properties which in many ways are more similar to things you find in the inorganic world, for unknown reasons. If this turns out to be on the right track, it would be even more remarkable in that same sense because the last thing you would expect of a biological system is that it would be anything like optimally designed.

DB *Is this input coming from students and colleagues?*

A lot of it's work of mine, but of course it's all highly interactive. These are all very cooperative enterprises. I have a course every fall which is a sort of lecture-seminar. People show up for it from all over the place. It's developed a certain pattern over the past thirty or forty years. A lot of faculty show up from other universities, other disciplines. There are many people who have been sitting in for twenty and thirty years, people from other universities. A lot of people come from the whole northeast region, from Canada and Maryland. There are plenty of European visitors. It's a very lively, ongoing sort of lecture-seminar. I lecture and then there's a lot of discussion. It's dealing with questions at the borders of research, always. Sometimes it's really interesting. Sometimes it's not so interesting. This last fall, in fact the last two years, particularly this fall, a lot of things fell together as I was lecturing. I'm writing them up right now.

DB *That's great. I'm excited for you, too, that you find your work engaging.*

I always find it engaging, but as I say, there's a rhythm. Sometimes it's more a matter of patchwork within a framework, and sometimes it's a matter of suddenly seeing another way of looking at things which seems to cut through a lot of problems and to have exciting prospects. This is maybe the most interesting thing I've thought of, at least. Whether it's right or not is another question.

DB *And given that, and this vital work that you're involved with, I was wondering if any thoughts of retiring come up.*

Sure. I have to at my age. And there are also questions about what's the best way of developing continuity in the department, and the impact on the field, and there's personal life, and so on. There are so many things I want to do. There's also the question of distribution of time and energy.

DB *How's your health?*

Fine.

DB *That's not a major consideration?*

No.

DB *Over the last few weeks I was rereading your book* Turning the Tide, *in particular the section on the right-wing counterattack and specifically the growth and power of right-wing institutions and foundations.*

That's interesting. I was just reading the same thing.

DB *You were?*

In fact, the article that I have in Z begins by referring back to some of the things that were going on in 1980 and 1984, those elections. It starts with some of my comments adapted from that very section. The analogy is so striking.

DB *That's what I thought, too. I wonder if the recent ...*

It's just like a repeat.

DB *The November 1994 election.*

But what happened, and the fraud about what happened are identical.

DB *The fraud being ...*

One of the points I made back then—this is in the mid-1980s—is that both the 1980 and the 1984 elections were called "conservative landslides," "great Reagan revolutions," etc. But in fact, what happened was quite different. The population was continuing to move away from Reaganite-type politics. Virtually no one in the general population saw what they call "conservatism" as an issue. It was 4% or 8% or something. Reagan, of course, had under a third of the electorate. But furthermore, of the voters, most of them wanted his legislative program not to be enacted because they opposed it. What was actually happening there was a vote against. People felt remote from the system, didn't like what was going on, opposed everything that was happening. Their own concerns and interests, which were sort of New Deal-style liberalism, roughly, were simply not being articulated at all in the political system, so they either didn't vote, or they voted against. But also, though maybe they liked Reagan's smile more than Mondale's frown, they also, of people who had an opinion, about 70% of the voters were opposed to Reagan's policies. Of the non-voters it was much higher.

That's pretty much what happened this time. The reason it was called a "conservative landslide" then was because elite groups wanted it that way. They wanted to tear apart the rather weak remnants of welfare state policies and redirect social policy even more than usual towards the interests of the powerful and the privileged. So that's what they wanted. That's the way they interpreted the vote. That's across the spectrum. That includes liberals for the most part. Pretty much the same is true now. So if you look at the latest vote, the 1992 vote and the 1994 vote were virtually identical, with a couple of percentage points difference, largely attributable to the fact that the voting was skewed even more toward the wealthy than is usual.

Among non-voters, who are, of course, the big majority, the overwhelming number call themselves "pro-democrat," but what they mean by "democrat" is something that wasn't represented in the current election. The opposition to "New Democrats" of the Clinton variety was much higher than to what are called "traditional" Democrats, traditional liberals. If you look at the outcome, the Democrats who tried to mobilize the traditional constituencies, like labor and women, they did rather well. The ones who got smashed were the Clinton-style "New Democrats." If you look at opinion polls, you can see why. Public opinion is overwhelmingly opposed to the policies that are shared by Gingrich and Clinton, on just about every issue. But most people simply don't feel themselves represented. When asked, for example, whether they thought that having a conservative Congress was an important issue, in this election, about 12% of voters said, Yes. Virtually no one, in other words. It's very similar to the early 1980s. The reason why it's described this way, I'm sure, is that these are the policies that the privileged and the powerful want. So they're going to claim that they have a popular mandate for them, even though they don't. It'll mean a further narrowing of the spectrum towards the right by choice. Not under popular pressure, but by choice of elites. That's what they want. And it's not surprising that they want it. It's good for them.

Clinton and his advisors decided to interpret the vote as meaning that they should move even further to an unpopular position than they already were, instead of interpreting it to mean, We ought to speak to the majority of the population who are opposed to what we're doing, and even more opposed to what the Republicans are doing. So they interpret it that way, despite their own polls, which showed the opposite, because that's the conclusion they want to draw.

DB *But tell me one thing: As I recall, in the 1980s, during the Reagan period, the elite corporate media pretty much welcomed Reaganomics and the whole Reagan program, whereas this time one reads in the* New York Times *and the* Washington Post *scathing critiques of Gingrich, really strong criticisms.*

That was before the election. It's toned down since then. The Gingrich program has several aspects to it. He wants to focus on what he calls "cultural issues." That makes sense, because when you're going to rob people blind you don't want to have them focus their attention on economic issues. The second is the actual programs, robbing people blind and enriching the rich. On those programs, I don't see that there is much opposition from the corporate media. For example, you read today's editorials. Did they condemn Clinton for yesterday announcing that he was going to make government leaner and cut back support for nuclear waste disposal and so on? I doubt it. I haven't read the papers yet.

What they do oppose, however, and are very upset about, is what they call the Gingrich-style "cultural offensive," because that in fact is attacking the values of the elite as well. I think there's a kind of internal contradiction there that elite groups are having a hard time coming to terms with. In order to push through the social policies that really interest them, like distributing resources even more to the rich than before and reducing the status of the general population and marginalizing them even more than before—in order to carry that off, they have to develop at least some kind of popular support. You have to mobilize some support for what you're doing. You can't do that on the social and economic issues. So therefore you turn to what they call "cultural issues." There's something that resembles the 1930s about this, Germany in the 1930s. You try to mobilize people on something else. So a large part of the focus of attention in the Gingrich program is what he calls "rebuilding American civilization," which means cutting back on rights of women, prayer in the schools, narrowing the spectrum of discussion, attacking civil liberties, and so on. Those are things that rich and powerful people don't like, because they benefit from those. First of all, they tend to be what is called "liberal" on cultural values. They want the kind of freedom that would be undermined if the Gingrich types actually were serious about this talk. So you get a kind of contradiction. You see it very clearly.

For example, the *New York Times* a couple of weeks ago had an editorial defending the counterculture.

DB *That was astounding.*

I didn't think it was astounding at all.

DB *You didn't?*

It was fairly natural. Because what they think of as the "counterculture" is what they themselves approve of. And if you did a poll among corporate executives, they would agree. They don't want to have their kids forced to pray in school. They don't want to have religious fundamentalists telling them what to do. They want their wives and daughters to have opportunities, abortion rights and other forms of freedom. They don't want to restore the kind of values, for themselves in their personal lives, that Gingrich is talking about. That's the kind of counterculture that they're defending. So I didn't think that it was surprising.

On the other hand, there was an even more dramatic article, I thought, a front-page story in the *Wall Street Journal* a couple of days ago which actually talked about "class war" and "economic classes." These are terms that are unusable in the U.S., but now they're using them. It's extremely interesting to see how they're putting it. They said that there is a class war developing between ordinary working-class blokes, that's one side, and they're an economic class—they said that—and then the elites who are oppressing them, who happen to be the liberals. The elites who are oppressing them are the elitist liberals with their crazy countercultural values. Who stands up for the ordinary working-class blokes? The so-called conservatives, who are in fact doing everything they can to destroy them. That's the class war. They apparently feel confident enough about their own takeover of the doctrinal system, which is also discussed in this 1985 book [*Turning the Tide*] that you mentioned. They feel confident enough about that that they're willing to even allow words like "class war" and "class conflict" as long as the ruling class is identified as the people who espouse these liberal, countercultural values. It's not a total perversion of reality. If you go to the actual, real ruling class, the people who own and invest and speculate and CEOs and the rest of them, they do generally share these so-called "liberal" values. That's why you find these rather striking internal contradictions, I think. On the one hand, Gingrich is following a propaganda line which is almost required if you want to be able to carry off a major attack against the population. But the elements of that propaganda line, at least taken literally, also strike at the interests of the rich and powerful. There is an internal contradiction there, and I think that's why you're seeing things like that *Times* editorial.

DB *That was on Sunday, December 11, 1994. I just want to mention one thing from that. They called the Vietnam policy "deranged."*

But you see, that's an old story.

DB *I don't recall them using that adjective during the period.*

That goes back to the early 1960s, when they were saying, These guys are crazy. They don't know how to win the war.

DB *So you think it's the pragmatists.*

Are they saying the aggression in South Vietnam was immoral? They're saying it was deranged. Look at this crazy thing—we were devoting our lives and energies and effort to save people who couldn't be saved because they were so valueless. That's back to David Halberstam in the early 1960s. The so-called critics were the people who said, You guys aren't doing it right. Anthony Lewis, when he finally became articulate against the war around 1970, said it began with blundering efforts to do good but ended up as a disaster. So it was deranged.

DB *More on this class war issue. If the Republican right-wing economic initiative, which is essentially an attack on the poor...*

"Poor" is a funny word for it. It's an attack on maybe three-quarters of the population.

DB *Might not elites be concerned in that it would result in social instability and uprisings like Los Angeles?*

That's why they have this huge crime bill, and they want to extend the crime bill. They want to criminalize a large part of the population. They have been working on this for some time. I think what's actually going on, in my opinion, if you go back to the 1970s, it began to appear, because of changes in the international economy, as if it might be possible for real ruling groups to do something that they've always hoped to do but couldn't, namely to roll back everything connected with the social contract that had been won by working people and poor people over a century of struggle. There was a kind of social contract. I think they think they can roll it back. They can go right back to the days of satanic mills (to use William Blake's phrase) where they believe they have enough weapons against the population—and it's not implausible—that they can destroy human rights, eliminate the curse of democracy, except in a purely formal way, move power into the hands of absolutist, unaccountable institutions which will run the world in their own interests, without looking at anyone else, enhance private power, and eliminate workers' rights, political rights, the right to food, destroy it all. Eliminate what used to be called the right to live. There was a battle about this in the early nineteenth century, and they couldn't quite carry it off. Now I think they think they can carry it off. That means in effect turning the industrialized countries into a kind of Third World, a kind of Latin America. That means for a sector of the population great wealth and privilege and enormous government protection, because none of these people believe in a free market or anything remotely like it. They want a powerful welfare state, directing resources and protection to them. So on the one hand you have a powerful welfare state for a small sector of the population. For the rest, those who you need to do the dirty work, you pay them a pittance, and if they won't do it, get somebody else. A large part of them are just superfluous. You don't need them at all. In the Third World, maybe you send out death squads. Here you don't quite send out death squads, so you lock them into urban slums which are more or less urban concentration camps and make sure they don't have any resources there so it will collapse and deteriorate. If that won't work, just throw them into jail.

DB *Do you see any resistance to these policies developing?*

Organized resistance? In a sense, but it's not constructive. For example, the vote in 1994 was a sort of resistance. It was an overwhelming vote against everything that's going on. But it didn't take a constructive form.

DB *61% of the population didn't vote.*

Yeah, but that's normal. Most people think it's all a joke. But even of those who voted, take a look at the minority who voted. I forget the exact numbers, but I think it was about 6 to 1 a vote against. Which is very similar to 1980, except that it's much more extreme now because we've had fifteen years of Reaganism. It started late in the Carter era, went through the Reagan years, and it's continuing through Clinton. That means a continuing increase in inequality, continuing literally the absolute reduction in standard of living for a majority of the population. It was stagnation for a while. It's been reduction since the 1980s. It's going down more during the Clinton years. What's remarkable now is that this is the first time ever, maybe, that during a period of economic recovery general living standards and economic standards have been declining. The Census Bureau just came out with figures for 1993, after two years of so-called recovery. The median income, where half is above, half below, has declined 7% since 1989. It's very unusual, maybe unprecedented for a recovery. Just this morning, did you get the *New York Times* this morning?

DB *Yeah, I've got it.*

Have a look. They report the Clinton budget cuts, etc. On the inside page, Section B, the continuation of the story, there's almost a full page devoted to the continuation of that. Then, on the right-hand column, there's an article reporting the latest conference of mayors. If you haven't read it, read it. It's interesting. The conference of mayors' report points out the number of people desperately needing food and housing has sharply increased. I think the numbers are in the range of 15% or something like that. A big proportion of them are simply being denied it because the cities don't have the resources. For that to be happening during a recovery—for that to be happening in a rich country is scandalous anyway. But for it to be happening in a period of recovery, an increase in starvation and homelessness, a sharp increase, enough that the conference of mayors made a report and did a bitter protest against federal policies, that's pretty astonishing.

People are aware that things are bad, but they don't have a constructive way to respond. For example, there's nothing in the political system. The polls and opinion studies and so on, including the exit polls after the last election, made it pretty clear what would be a winning policy in the political arena, namely, something that has a kind of populist, reformist, social democratic-type character. That would probably get a large majority of the population, judging by public attitudes. But nobody is going to say that, because they all want something else.

It was kind of interesting during the campaign to see how both sides covered up some very striking issues. Take, say, Newt Gingrich, who is just smashing the Democrats with all of his talk about a "nanny state" and a welfare state and get the government off our backs and you guys have been ruining the world with your nanny state. He was killing the Democrats with this. I couldn't find one person, either in the so-called liberal press or among the Democrats themselves, who made the obvious rejoinder: You're the biggest advocate in the country of the nanny state, or certainly one of the biggest ones. As I think you know, Gingrich's constituency, his district, gets more federal subsidies than any suburban county in the country outside the federal system.

DB *That's Cobb County, right outside of Atlanta.*

Take away Arlington, Virginia, which is part of Washington, and the Florida home of the Kennedy Space Center, and Cobb County is first. That's the nanny state. They are the beneficiaries of social policies which direct public resources toward the rich. A lot of it is through the Pentagon, which has that domestic function.

DB *Lockheed is based in Cobb County.*

Lockheed is their main employer. Besides that it's mainly things like computers and electronics, which is very heavily public-subsidized, and insurance. Why is insurance a place where you can make a lot of money? It's because the social policy is to ensure that private power, meaning insurance companies, runs huge programs. The most striking is the health program. That's public policy. Sane countries don't have that. So his constituency is in fact the beneficiaries of the nanny state to an extent beyond probably any other in the country outside the federal system.

To get back to my point, no Democrat pointed this out that I could see. And the reason is, I suspect, that they agree. They don't want to expose that, even at the cost of seriously losing elections and control of Congress.

Rollback

The Return of Predatory Capitalism

January 31 and February 3, 1995

DB *You just came back from a trip to Australia. Was it your first visit to the country?*

It was indeed my first visit to Australia. I was there for eight or nine days, a pretty constant schedule of talks and interviews, the usual stuff. There was the usual range of topics with enormous and very interested audiences. There was a lot of radio and television. The main invitation was from the East Timor Relief Association. There's a substantial Timorese community there. I gave talks primarily on East Timor. That was one major focus. And of course on Australia's policies towards East Timor and other things, also domestic economic policies.

The timing turned out to be very propitious. A major case opened at the World Court yesterday. I haven't seen it reported here, but it's being reported widely in the world press and of course extensively in Australia. The case involves Portugal and Australia. It has to do with the robbery of the oil of East Timor in a treaty signed between Australia and Indonesia. One primary reason (we know from leaked diplomatic cables and so on) for the Western support for the Indonesian invasion of East Timor, which was sort of near genocidal, was the fact that they thought they could make a better deal on robbing the oil resources with Indonesia than they could either with Portugal, which was the administering power, or an independent East Timor. That was stated very explicitly in diplomatic cables during the period when the governments were pretending that they didn't know that the invasion was imminent. But of course they did know. So that's a big issue now. Both the World Court hearing and the very fact that this is taking place, which is kind of as if Libya had made a deal with Iraq to exploit Kuwait's oil when they hadn't been driven out. It's roughly like that. So that was one big issue. And since it is just coming up to the World Court, that was timely.

The other thing was that, in fact as I landed at the airport, the first headline that greeted me in the national newspaper, *The Australian*, was that Australia agreed to sell advanced assault rifles to Indonesia, which of course are not to be used to defend Indonesia from China. They're being used for internal repression and the military occupation of East Timor, where the fighting is still going on and the repression is very severe. The point is that Australia found a niche market, because the U.S. had backed away from that, finally, under lots of pressure here, Congressional and popular pressure. The U.S. finally got to the point of withholding some arms, at least small arms, from the killers. Australia instantly moved in. The cynicism of that is a little hard to miss. You have to remember people in Australia know, even if they don't read about it in schoolbooks, but they remember, that about 60,000 Timorese were killed during the Second World War. The island of Timor was divided, half was a Portuguese colony and half was Dutch. The Portuguese part would have probably remained neutral through the war, like Macao, which was another Portuguese colony. Japan never violated its neutrality. Portugal was a fascist country. It was a semi-ally. So chances are Timor would have remained neutral. Anyhow, Australia invaded, and about ten days after Pearl Harbor the Japanese counter-invaded. There were a couple hundred Australian commandos there. They were able to survive, the ones that did, mostly because of assistance from Timorese. Otherwise they would have been wiped out instantly. Then they finally were withdrawn, but of course the Timorese were left. The ones that the Japanese thought had supported them were totally slaughtered. That fighting on Timor—if you look at the geography you'll see how it works. The Japanese might well have gone on to invade Australia. In fact they were going to. They never did. They bombed, but they never invaded. And probably the fighting on Timor stopped them. So 60,000 Timorese dead certainly saved a lot of lives of Australian commandos, and may have saved Australia from being invaded.

To repay that debt by being the only country in the world to officially recognize the occupation, to steal their oil, to arm the murderers, doesn't go over very well in the population. And there's also been tremendous cynicism in the government in justifying this. There's a kind of backlog of resentment and concern, plus the fact that it's right next door, so they get Timorese refugees. So it's a big issue.

DB *You also gave a presentation on anarchy. Is there a lively anarchist movement in Australia?*

I'm not in much of a position to say. The meeting was at the town hall in Sydney. There were a couple of thousand people there, and it was overflowing. They had had an all-day conference with plenty of people, so something's lively. You know what these trips are like, you run from one talk to another. I can't really comment on what the movements are like.

DB *I had a glimpse of what you go through. In November I was in Seattle and Olympia. I gave three public talks, three interviews, and a workshop in a day and a half. At the end of that time, my brains were completely fried. I had no idea what I'd said to whom. I was wondering, how do you keep not just your equilibrium and equanimity, but that separation of what you said?*

As far as I know, I have only one talent. I'm not trying to be modest. I think I know what I'm good at and what I'm not good at. The one talent that I have which I know many other friends don't seem to have is I've got some quirk in my brain which makes it work like separate buffers in a computer. If you play around with a computer you know you can put things in different places and they just stay there and you can go back to them whenever you feel like it and they're there. I can somehow do that. I can write a very technical paper in snatches: a piece on an airplane, another piece three weeks later, six months later finally get back to it and pick up where I left off. Somehow I don't have any problem switching very quickly from one thing to another. I have some other friends like this. I had one, a well-known logician in Israel, who was a very close friend. We would see each other every five or six years. We would always just pick up the conversation where we had left it off, without any break, without even noticing it, particularly. We didn't even notice it until people seemed to find it strange.

DB *Did your thoughts while you were in Australia ever turn to Alex Carey, the man you dedicated* Manufacturing Consent *to?*

Very much so. In fact, I was there for a book launch. His book of posthumous essays, *Taking the Risk Out of Democracy*, was published by the University of New South Wales, where he taught. I wrote an introduction to it, in fact. One of the things I did was to go to the launch of the book and talk about it a bit and meet the family. I also met some old friends who I knew through and with Alex when he visited here years back, so there was a lot of personal stuff, too.

DB *What's memorable about his work? What was his contribution?*

Alex Carey did the pioneering work in an extremely important field which in fact has yet to be investigated. That's the field of corporate propaganda, which is a major phenomenon in the modern world and almost unstudied. His most important essay "Changing Public Opinion: The Corporate Offensive," which has been circulating underground for years (I've duplicated and circulated endless copies myself) was never published in his lifetime. It's in the new collection. It opens by pointing out—he says it better than this—that there have been three major phenomena in the twentieth century with regard to democracy. One is the extension of the franchise, which was broad. The second was the growth of corporations. The third was the growth of corporate propaganda to undermine democracy. And he's exactly right. That's why we have a public relations industry. It was established approximately at the time that corporations reached their current form early in the century. It was created in order, as they put it, to "control the public mind," because they recognized that the public mind would be the greatest hazard facing industrialists, and they understood that democracy is a real threat to private tyranny, just as it's a threat to state tyranny. Now, we are in a system of private tyranny, which was being established early in the century, and very consciously so. In fact it was consciously established as an attack on individual liberty. That's a part of corporate law which is only known in scholarly circles.

Part of this was to ensure that democracy couldn't function. And since you have some degree of state violence, but limited degrees, especially with the increase in the franchise and participation, it was understood right off that you have to control opinion. That led to the huge public relations industry and massive propaganda campaigns, efforts to sell Americanism and harmony and to sell American capitalism. People are deluged with propaganda on this through the Advertising Council and radio and television and other media. It's very conscious. Carey is the first person to have seriously studied it, and almost the last person. Now there's a little literature on it coming along, primarily an excellent study called *Selling Free Enterprise*, by Elizabeth Fones-Wolf published by the University of Illinois Press, focusing on the post-World War II period. Fones-Wolf adds a great deal of new material on the extraordinary scale of the propaganda efforts "to indoctrinate people with the capitalist story," and the dedicated self-consciousness with which "the everlasting battle for the minds of men" was pursued. It's a topic of such incredible significance in the twentieth century that it ought to be a major focus. We are immersed in it all the time. It explains a lot. The U.S. is different from other countries in this respect. It has a much more class-conscious business community, for all kinds of historical reasons. It didn't develop out of feudalism and aristocracy. So there weren't the conflicting factors you had in other places—the highly class-conscious business community, very Marxist in character, vulgar Marxist, fighting a bitter class war, and very aware of it. You read internal publications and it's like reading Maoist pamphlets half the time. They don't spend billions of dollars a year on propaganda for the fun of it. They do it with a purpose. For a long time the purpose was to resist and contain human rights and democracy and the whole welfare state framework, the social contract, that developed over the years. They wanted to contain it and limit it. Now they feel, in the current period, that they can really roll it back. They'd go right back to satanic mills, murdering poor people, basically the social structure of the early nineteenth century. That's the situation we're in right now. These huge propaganda offensives are a major part of it.

The real importance of Carey's work is that it's the first effort and until now the major effort to bring some of this to public attention. It's had a tremendous influence on the work I've done. Ed Herman and I dedicated our book, *Manufacturing Consent*, to him. He had just died. It was not intended as just a symbolic gesture. He got both of us started in a lot of this work.

DB *You just mentioned "rollback." It's also the title of a series of essays in Z magazine that you just wrote. That was originally a Cold War term.*

I picked it up from there. The standard line, if you read the Clinton Doctrine as announced by Anthony Lake, the intellectual in the administration, is that for years we've been involved in containment of a threat to market democracy. Now we're going to enlarge it. So he's picking Cold War imagery. And I think that Cold War imagery is appropriate, except that he's got it backwards. For years we've been involved in *containment* of democracy, freedom, human rights, and even markets, and now we're going to be able to roll them back. "Rollback" is another Cold War term, as you mentioned. The traditional Cold War policies were that we oscillate between containment and rollback. Containment is Kennan's policy. You prevent the Soviet power from expanding. That's containment.

Rollback has been, in fact, official U.S. policy since 1950. NSC-68, the core Cold War doctrine, is an advocacy of rollback. That's when Kennan was thrown out and Nitze and others came in. Rollback meant we undermine and destroy Soviet power and we reach negotiations with "a successor state or states," as the NSC put it. These traditional international Cold War notions are, I think, very appropriate, except that they're misplaced. Containment is in fact correct, but it wasn't containment of a Soviet threat. It was containment of the threat of freedom, democracy, human rights, other threats to authority. And now they feel they can move on to roll back and unravel the entire social contract which developed through large-scale popular struggle over a century and a half, which did sort of soften the edges of predatory private tyranny, and often softened them a lot. In Germany, for example, workers have fairly reasonable conditions. So that has to be rolled back, and we have to go back to the days when we had wage slavery, as it was called by working people in the nineteenth century. No rights. The only rights you get are the rights you gain on the labor market. If your children can't make enough money to survive, they starve. Your choices are the workhouse prison, the labor market, whatever you can get there. Or, if you go back to the early days of the 1820s, the line was, "Or go somewhere else." Meaning, go to the places where white settlers are massacring the indigenous populations and opening them up, like the U.S. and Australia, for example.

Of course, now that option is gone. You don't go somewhere else. So the choices are limited to the other two, as the founders of modern economics, like Ricardo and Malthus and others, pointed out: workhouse prison or starvation, or whatever you can gain on the labor market. You don't have any rights on the labor market. It's just a market. That in fact is the foundation of the intellectual tradition that is called classical economics now, neoliberalism, and so on.

The idea is to go right back to those choices, with one crucial difference. There's a little secret that everybody knows but you're not supposed to say, and that is that nobody who advocated this believed a word of it. They always wanted a very powerful state which intervenes massively, but it's a welfare state for the rich. That's the way the U.S. was founded. In fact, the U.S. pioneered that development. It's been the most protectionist of all the industrial societies. It's a well-known fact. Alexander Hamilton is the one who invented the concept of infant industry protection and modern protectionism. The U.S. has always been a pioneer and a bastion of protectionism, which is why it's a rich, powerful country. Another slight secret of economic history, again well known to scholars, is that the free market policies have been an utter disaster. Anyone who is subjected to them gets smashed, which is why the Third World looks the way it is. They were forced on the Third World. And every single developed society has radically violated those principles, the U.S. more than most. That's closely correlated with growth. If you look historically, protectionism is actually correlated with trade, even. The more protectionism, the more trade, for a simple reason: protectionism enhances growth, and growth enhances trade. That was generally true over quite a long period. And protectionism is only one form of state intervention.

For poor people and working people, they have to be subjected to market discipline. That part is true. But the other side, which is less said, is that rich people are going to have a nanny state protecting and subsidizing them, and a powerful one.

DB *One of the heroes of the current right-wing revival—I'm not going to use the term "conservative"—is Adam Smith. You've done some pretty impressive research on Smith that has excavated, as the postmodernists would say, a lot of information that's not coming out. You've often quoted him describing the "vile maxim of the masters of mankind: all for ourselves and nothing for other people."*

I didn't do any research at all on Smith. I just read him. There's no research. Just read it. He's pre-capitalist, a figure of the Enlightenment. What we would call capitalism he despised. People read snippets of Adam Smith, the few phrases they teach in school. Everybody reads the first paragraph of *The Wealth of Nations* where he talks about how wonderful the division of labor is. But not many people get to the point hundreds of pages later, where he says that division of labor will destroy human beings and turn them into creatures as stupid and ignorant as it is possible for a human being to be. And therefore in any civilized society the government is going to have to take some measures to prevent division of labor from proceeding to its limits.

He did give an argument for markets, but the argument was that under conditions of perfect liberty, markets will lead to perfect equality. That's the argument for them, because he thought equality of condition (not just opportunity) is what you should be aiming at. It goes on and on. He gave a devastating critique of what we would call North-South policies. He was talking about England and India. He bitterly condemned the British experiments they were carrying out which were devastating India.

He also made remarks which ought to be truisms about the way states work. He pointed out that it's totally senseless to talk about a nation and what we would nowadays call "national interests." He simply observed in passing, because it's so obvious, that in England, which is what he's discussing—and it was the most democratic society of the day—the principal architects of policy are the "merchants and manufacturers," and they make certain that their own interests are, in his words, "most peculiarly attended to," no matter what the effect on others, including the people of England, who, he argued, suffered from their policies. He didn't have the data to prove it at the time, but he was probably right.

This truism was a century later called class analysis, but you don't have to go to Marx to find it. It's very explicit in Adam Smith. It's so obvious that any ten-year-old can see it. So he didn't make a big point of it. He just mentioned it. But that's correct. If you read through his work, he's intelligent. He's a person who was from the Enlightenment. His driving motives were the assumption that people are guided by sympathy and feelings of solidarity and the need for control of their own work, much like other Enlightenment and early Romantic thinkers. He's part of that period, the Scottish Enlightenment.

The version of him that's given today is just ridiculous. But I didn't have to do any research to find this out. All you have to do is read. If you're literate, you'll find it out. I did do a little research in the way it's treated, and that's interesting. For example, the University of Chicago, the great bastion of free market economics, etc., etc., published a bicentennial edition of the hero, a scholarly edition with all the footnotes and the introduction by a Nobel Prize winner, George Stigler, a huge index, a real scholarly edition. That's the one I used. It's the best edition. The scholarly framework was very interesting, including Stigler's introduction. It's likely he never opened *The Wealth of Nations*. Just about everything he said about the book was completely false. I went through a bunch of examples in writing about it, in *Year 501* and elsewhere.

But even more interesting in some ways was the index. Adam Smith is very well known for his advocacy of division of labor. Take a look at "division of labor" in the index and there are lots and lots of things listed. But there's one missing, namely his denunciation of division of labor, the one I just cited. That's somehow missing from the index. It goes on like this. I wouldn't call this research, because it's ten minutes' work, but if you look at the scholarship, then it's interesting.

I want to be clear about this. There is good Smith scholarship. If you look at the serious Smith scholarship, nothing I'm saying is any surprise to anyone. How could it be? You open the book and you read it and it's staring you right in the face. On the other hand, if you look at the myth of Adam Smith, which is the only one we get, the discrepancy between that and the reality is enormous.

This is true of classical liberalism in general. The founders of classical liberalism, people like Adam Smith and Wilhelm von Humboldt, who is one of the great exponents of classical liberalism, and who inspired John Stuart Mill—they were what we would call libertarian socialists, at least that's the way I read them. For example, Humboldt, like Smith, says, Consider a craftsman who builds some beautiful thing. Humboldt says if he does it under external coercion, like pay, for wages, we may admire what he does but we will despise what he is. On the other hand, if he does it out of his own free, creative expression of himself, under free will, not under external coercion of wage labor, then we also admire what he is because he's a human being. He said any decent socioeconomic system will be based on the assumption that people have the freedom to inquire and create—since that's the fundamental nature of humans—in free association with others, but certainly not under the kinds of external constraints that later came to be called capitalism.

It's the same when you read Jefferson. He lived a half century later, so he saw state capitalism developing, and he despised it, of course. He said it's going to lead to a form of absolutism worse than the one we defended ourselves against. In fact, if you run through this whole period you see a very clear, sharp critique of what we would later call capitalism and certainly of the twentieth-century version of it, which is designed in fact to destroy individual, even entrepreneurial capitalism.

There's a side current here which is rarely looked at but which is also quite fascinating. That's the working class literature of the nineteenth century. They didn't read Adam Smith and Wilhelm von Humboldt, but they're saying the same things. Read journals put out by the people called the "factory girls of Lowell," young women in the factories, mechanics, and other working people who were running their own newspapers. It's the same kind of critique. There was a real battle fought by working people in England and the U.S. to defend themselves against what they called the degradation and oppression and violence of the industrial capitalist system, which was not only dehumanizing them but was even radically reducing their intellectual level. So you go back to the mid-nineteenth century and these so-called "factory girls," young girls working in the Lowell mills, were reading serious contemporary literature. They recognized that the point of the system was to turn them into tools who would be manipulated, degraded, kicked around, and so on. And they fought against it bitterly for a long period. That's the history of the rise of capitalism.

The other part of the story is the development of corporations, which is an interesting story in itself. Adam Smith didn't say much about them, but he did criticize the early stages of them. Jefferson lived long enough to see the beginnings, and he was very strongly opposed to them. But the development of corporations really took place in the early twentieth century and very late in the nineteenth century. Originally corporations existed as a public service. People would get together to build a bridge and they would be incorporated for that purpose by the state. They built the bridge and that's it. They were supposed to have a public interest function. Well into the 1870s, states were removing corporate charters. They were granted by the state. They didn't have any other authority. They were fictions. They were removing corporate charters because they weren't serving a public function. But then you get into the period of trusts and various efforts to consolidate power that were beginning to be made in the late nineteenth century. It's interesting to look at the literature. The courts didn't really accept it. There were some hints about it. It wasn't until the early twentieth century that courts and lawyers designed a new socioeconomic system. It was never done by legislation. It was done mostly by courts and lawyers and the power they could exercise over individual states. New Jersey was the first state that granted corporations any right they wanted. Of course, all the capital in the country suddenly started to flow to New Jersey, for obvious reasons. Then the other states had to do the same thing just to defend themselves or be wiped out. It's kind of a small-scale globalization. Then the courts and the corporate lawyers came along and created a whole new body of doctrine which gave corporations authority and power that they had never had before. If you look at the background of it, it's the same background that led to fascism and Bolshevism. A lot of it was supported by people called progressives, for these reasons: They said, individual rights are gone. We are in a period of corporatization of power, consolidation of power, centralization. That's supposed to be good if you're a progressive, like a Marxist-Leninist. Out of that same background came three major things: fascism, Bolshevism, and corporate tyranny. They all grew out of the same more or less Hegelian roots. It's fairly recent. We think of corporations as immutable, but they were designed. It's a conscious design which worked as Adam Smith said: the principal architects of policy consolidate state power and use it for their interests. It was certainly not popular will. It's basically court decisions and lawyers' decisions, which created a form of private tyranny which is now more massive in many ways than even state tyranny was. These are major parts of modern twentieth-century history. The classical liberals would be horrified. They didn't even imagine this. But the smaller things that they saw, they were already horrified about. This would have totally scandalized Adam Smith or Jefferson or anyone like that.

DB *Let's make a connection between corporations and East Timor and Indonesia. Nike is the world's largest manufacturer of sneakers and sportswear. It's headquarters is in Beaverton, Oregon, right outside of Portland. Some years ago they had set up factories in South Korea. South Korean workers started unionizing and demanding better pay and better working conditions. Nike moved their operations to Indonesia, where they* *pay workers $1.35 a day. Nike makes these sneakers in Indonesia for $5.40 and sells them in the U.S. for $60, $70, $80.*

Indonesia has been a great favorite of the West, ever since 1965, when a huge massacre took place. They slaughtered maybe half a million or so people and destroyed the one popular political party there, which was, as everyone from right to left agrees, defending the interests of the poor. This slaughter was welcomed with absolute euphoria in the West. I've reviewed some of the press coverage. Since Indonesia is a pretty rich country, lots of resources, it's what's been called a "paradise" for investors. It is a brutal, repressive state which prevents any labor organizing or anything else, so wages can be very low. Indonesian wages are now half the level of China, which is not exactly high. At the 1994 APEC conference, everybody went to Jakarta to celebrate the free market. As part of cleaning the place up, they threw all the labor leaders in jail. Some of them are in there for long sentences. Some of the sentences have just been increased. They don't tolerate labor unions. There's a Stalinist-style labor union run by the government. There have been attempts to create independent unions, but they have been brutally suppressed. So Nike's happy, because the work force is—although they're very militant and very courageous—brutally repressed by the state and kept way down. The country's extremely rich. There's a lot of wealth around, mostly in the hands of General Suharto and his family and their cronies and foreign investors.

Even the invasion of East Timor, as I've mentioned, was motivated to a substantial extent by corporate robbery. A large part of the reason can be seen in an important leak of diplomatic cables from right before the invasion, around August 1975. These Australian cables first of all talked directly about the complicity of the U.S., of Kissinger ordering the Jakarta Embassy not to report any more on what's going on because the U.S. was going to support the invasion, as it did. Of course they publicly denied knowing anything about it. The Australian Ambassador said, his words were something like this, We can make a better deal on East Timorese oil with Indonesia than we can with Portugal, the administering power, or with an independent East Timor. In fact, that is now exactly what's going on. A few years later Australia recognized the occupation, the only Western country to recognize it, in the context of negotiations with Indonesia about the Timor Gap Treaty. There was a big massacre in Dili in 1991 which did focus the world's attention on the occupation. A couple hundred people were murdered by Indonesian troops who made the mistake of doing it in front of a hidden television camera and beating up two American reporters. You're not supposed to do things like that. You're supposed to do massacres in secret while nobody's looking. They made that technical error, so there was a lot of coverage for a while. Immediately after that—and here the coverage declines, I have yet to see a word about it in the U.S., maybe in some of the business press—Australia and Indonesia granted licenses to major oil companies to begin drilling for Timorese oil. You have to recall that the official reason given as to why East Timor can't be independent is that it doesn't have any resources. That reason is given by the people who are robbing it of its oil resources, which are expected to be quite substantial.

As I mentioned, there is now a World Court case in process right now—that you really don't see coverage of. It's on kind of technical issues. The World Court isn't going to deal with the question of whether a country favored by the West is allowed to occupy and massacre other people. That's beyond courts. But they will look at the technical side. The London *Financial Times*, a major business journal, just had a big article on January 30th timed with the opening of the World Court hearing, describing it as one of the most important court trials ever, because it is going to establish the basis for commercial exploitation or, to be more accurate, robbery of the resources of a conquered people. It's a major issue. That's quite apart from the fact that with U.S. assistance Indonesia managed to slaughter maybe a quarter of the population, a couple hundred thousand people. And it's still going on.

DB *I'd like to put readers in this office space for a moment. Your desk is pretty neat right now. There are usually even higher piles of books. There are at least six or seven piles, stacks of books and papers, and on your filing cabinets even more. How do you divide your labor? You've just been away for about two weeks. You come back and have this avalanche of mail, phone calls, things to read. How do you get through this? What are you prioritizing here? Is there an order to this madness?*

First of all, it looks remarkably neat now because while I was away they did something really nasty. They painted and cleaned the office, which I never would have permitted while I was here. So it looks surprisingly clean. You may have noticed I'm trying to take care of that. So it does look neater than usual. But if you want to know what it's like, you've been at our house. Around 4:30 this morning there was what we thought was an earthquake, a huge noise. Our bedroom's right next to the study. We went in and discovered that these big piles of books, six feet high, a couple of piles had fallen and were scattered all over the floor. That's where I put the books that are urgent reading. Sometimes when I've having an extremely boring phone call, I try to calculate how many centuries I'd have to live in order to read the urgent books if I were to read twenty-four hours a day, seven days a week at some speed reading pace. It's pretty depressing. So the answer to your question is, I don't get anywhere near doing what I would like to do.

DB *Just in the last year or so you've written introductions to Paul Farmer's book (*The Uses of Haiti*) on Haiti, Jennifer Harbury's book (*Bridge of Courage*) on Guatemala, the Frederic Clairmont book on world trade.*

And Alex Carey's book, and several books of my own, a lot of articles, plus all the linguistics, which is a totally different thing. On the way back from Australia, it's a long flight, about seventeen or eighteen hours, I spent it all proofreading a very technical manuscript on a totally different topic. Plus I have a couple articles coming out in *Mind* and other philosophy journals.

DB *Those long flights must provide at least a sense of respite for you because you're not bombarded with telephone calls and people like me knocking on the door.*

One thing that surprised me in Australia, and I hope it doesn't come here, is that they're very high tech in some ways that we aren't. So everybody had a mobile phone. As we were driving around in cars there were phone calls going up and back. One thing I've always liked about driving, like flying, is that you're inaccessible. But apparently not any longer. Flying is very good in that respect. You're totally anonymous. Nobody can bother you.

DB *One of the things I've observed over the years of working with* *you and watching you interact with others is a sense of balance and enormous patience. You're very patient with people, particularly people who ask the most inane kinds of questions. Is this something you've cultivated?*

First of all, I'm usually fuming inside, so what you see on the outside isn't necessarily what's inside. But as far as questions, the only thing I ever get irritated about is elite intellectuals, the stuff they do I do find irritating. I shouldn't. I should expect it. But I do find it irritating. But on the other hand, what you're describing as inane questions usually strike me as perfectly honest questions. People have no reason to believe anything other than what they're saying. If you think about where the questioner is coming from, what the person has been exposed to, that's a very rational and intelligent question. It may sound inane from some other point of view, but it's not at all inane from within the framework in which it's being raised. It's usually quite reasonable. So there's nothing to be irritated about.

You may be sorry about the conditions in which the questions arise. The thing to do is to try to help them get out of their intellectual confinement, which is not just accidental, as I mentioned. There are huge efforts that do go into making people, to borrow Adam Smith's phrase, "as stupid and ignorant as it's possible for a human being to be." A lot of the educational system is designed for that, if you think about it, it's designed for obedience and passivity. From childhood, a lot of it is designed to prevent people from being independent and creative. If you're independent-minded in school, you're probably going to get in trouble very early on. That's not the trait that's being preferred or cultivated. When people live through all this stuff, plus corporate propaganda, plus television, plus the press and the whole mass, the deluge of ideological distortion that goes on, they ask questions that from another point of view sound inane, but from their point of view are completely reasonable.

DB *You either have ESP or you've been looking at my notes, because I was going to ask you a question about education. You're fond of quoting an anecdote of a former colleague of yours at MIT, Vicky Weisskopf.*

Vicky Weisskopf, who just retired, is a very famous physicist. One of the good things about this place is that the senior faculty teach introductory courses. He used to teach introductory physics courses.

He's one of the most distinguished physicists of the twentieth century, not a minor figure. The story—I don't know whether it's true or not—is that students would ask him, What are we going to cover in the course? His answer always was that the question is not what we're going to cover, but what we're going to *dis*cover. In other words, it doesn't matter what coverage there is. What matters is whether you learn to think independently. If so, you can find the material and the answers yourself. Anyone who teaches science, at least at an advanced level, is perfectly aware of the fact that you don't lecture. You may be standing in front of a room, but it's a cooperative enterprise. Studying is more a form of apprenticeship than anything else. It's kind of like learning to be a skilled carpenter. You work with somebody who knows how to do it. Sometimes you get it, sometimes you don't get it. If you get it, you're a skilled carpenter. How it's transmitted, nobody can say. Science is a lot like that. You just sort of have to get it. The way you get it is by interacting. The same is true here. You go to a class in linguistics and it's a discussion. The people sitting in the seat where you're sitting are usually so-called students who are talking about things, teaching me about what they've discovered. That was Weisskopf's point.

DB *At the Mellon lecture that you gave in Chicago in October, you focused primarily on the ideas of John Dewey and Bertrand Russell. It was very different from one of your political talks, for obvious reasons. Not to say you're not engaged in the political analysis as well, but there was really a different tone and timbre to your voice. There was a certain intellectual excitement when you were talking about these ideas that really matter to you and from what you said influenced you a great deal.*

They did. Not so much by reading as by living. From about eighteen months old, both my parents were working, and I was in what was called school. It happened to be an experimental school run by Temple University on Deweyite lines. So until I was about twelve years old I just experienced Deweyite ideas, rather well executed, incidentally. Progressive education isn't what's called that, but this was the real stuff. It was an exciting period. Later I read the thinking behind it. I didn't read about it when I was eight years old. I just lived it. These were highly libertarian ideas. Dewey himself comes straight from the American mainstream. People who read what he actually said would now consider him some far-out anti-American lunatic or something. He was expressing mainstream thinking before the ideological system had so grotesquely distorted the tradition. By now it's unrecognizable. For example, not only did he agree with the whole Enlightenment tradition that, as he put it, "the goal of production is to produce free people," ("free *men*," he said, but that's many years ago). That's the goal of production, not to produce commodities. He was a major theorist of democracy. There were many different, conflicting strands to democratic theory, but the one I'm talking about held that democracy requires dissolution of private power. He said as long as there is private control over the economic system, talk about democracy is a joke. Repeating basically Adam Smith, Dewey said, Politics is the shadow that big business casts over society. He said attenuating the shadow doesn't do much. Reforms are still going to leave it tyrannical. Basically a classical liberal view. His main point was that you can't even talk about democracy until you have democratic control of industry, commerce, banking, everything. That means control by the people who work in the institutions, and the communities.

These are standard libertarian socialist and anarchist ideas which go straight back to the Enlightenment, an outgrowth of the views of the kind that we were talking about before from classical liberalism. Dewey represented these in the modern period, as did Bertrand Russell, from another tradition, but again with roots in the Enlightenment. These were two of the major, if not the two major thinkers, of the twentieth century, whose ideas are about as well known as those of the real Adam Smith. Which is a sign of how efficient the educational system has been, and the propaganda system, in simply destroying even our awareness of our own immediate intellectual background.

DB *In that same Mellon lecture, you paraphrased Russell on education. You said that he promoted the idea that education is not to be viewed as something like filling a vessel with water, but rather assisting a flower to grow in its own way. That's poetic.*

That's an eighteenth-century idea. I don't know if Russell knew about it or re-invented it, but you read that as standard in early Enlightenment literature. That's the image that was used. That's essentially what Weisskopf was saying, too. Humboldt, the founder of classical liberalism, his view was that education is a matter of laying out a string along which the child will develop, but in its own way. You may do some guiding. That's what serious education would be, from kindergarten up through graduate school. You do get it in advanced science, because there's no other way to do it.

But most of the educational system is quite different. Mass education was designed to turn independent farmers into docile, passive tools of production. That was its primary purpose. And don't think people didn't know it. They knew it and they fought against it. There was a lot of resistance to mass education for exactly that reason. It was also understood by the elites. Emerson once said something about how we're educating them to keep them from our throats. If you don't educate them, what we call "education," they're going to take control—"they" being what Alexander Hamilton called the "great beast," namely the people. The anti-democratic thrust of opinion in what are called democratic societies is really ferocious. And for good reasons. Because the freer the society gets, the more dangerous the great beast becomes and the more you have to be careful to cage it somehow.

On the other hand, there are exceptions, and Dewey and Russell are among those exceptions. But they are completely marginalized and unknown, although everybody sings praises to them, as they do to Adam Smith. What they actually said would be considered intolerable in the autocratic climate of dominant opinion. The totalitarian element of it is quite striking. The very fact that the concept "anti-American" can exist—forget the way it's used—exhibits a totalitarian streak that's pretty dramatic. That concept, anti-Americanism—the only real counterpart to it in the modern world is anti-Sovietism. In the Soviet Union, the worst crime was to be anti-Soviet. That's the hallmark of a totalitarian society, to have concepts like anti-Sovietism or anti-Americanism. Here it's considered quite natural. Books on anti-Americanism, by people who are basically Stalinist clones, are highly respected. That's true of Anglo-American societies, which are strikingly the more democratic societies. I think there's a correlation there. That's basically Alex Carey's point. As freedom grows, the need to coerce and control opinion also grows if you want to prevent the great beast from doing something with its freedom.

DB *These qualities that I think you're looking for and want to elicit from your students, a sense of inquiry, skepticism, challenging you, maybe* *just saying, You're a nice guy but you don't know what you're talking about, how do you foster those? You come in with a certain amount of baggage into a classroom. People say, This is Noam Chomsky, the father of modern linguistics and all that. Do you find students are in awe of you or are hesitant to speak out?*

Not most. Most of them are pretty independent-minded. And they soon pick up the atmosphere around. Walk around and you'll see. It's a very informal atmosphere of interchange and cooperation. These are ideals, of course. You may not live up to them properly, but it's certainly what everyone is committed to. There are students who find it harder, especially ones who come from Asian backgrounds. They've had a much more authoritarian tradition. Some of them break through quite quickly, some don't. But by and large the people who make it into elite graduate programs are that tiny minority who haven't had the creativity and independence beaten out of them. It doesn't work 100%.

There was some interesting stuff written about this by Sam Bowles and Herb Gintis, two economists, in their work on the American educational system some years back. They pointed out that the educational system is divided into fragments. The part that's directed towards working people and the general population is indeed designed to impose obedience. But the education for elites can't quite do that. It has to allow creativity and independence. Otherwise they won't be able to do their job of making money. You find the same thing in the press. That's why I read the *Wall Street Journal* and the *Financial Times* and *Business Week*. They just have to tell the truth. That's a contradiction in the mainstream press, too. Take, say, the *New York Times* or the *Washington Post*. They have dual functions, and they're contradictory. One function is to subdue the great beast. But another function is to let their audience, which is an elite audience, gain a tolerably realistic picture of what's going on in the world. Otherwise they won't be able to satisfy their own needs. That's a contradiction that runs right through the educational system as well. It's totally independent of another factor, namely just professional integrity, which a lot of people have: honesty, no matter what the external constraints are. That leads to various complexities. If you really look at the details of how the newspapers work, you find these contradictions and problems playing themselves out in complicated ways.

DB *Do you find that when you're doing these one-on-one's with the students in your office that they're more open and communicate more easily with you than in class?*

My classes have a funny property. They've become a kind of institution. There's the Thursday afternoon seminar. The participants are from all over the place, as we discussed earlier, including faculty from several fields and many places and more advanced students who may have taken the course officially before. Actual students are a small minority and sometimes tend to be somewhat intimidated. The discussions are mostly among faculty. What I've done over the years is to break the class into two, so there's two and a half hours of free-floating interchange with everyone. Then everybody gets kicked out and only the actual students are left. These are just discussion sections, which the actual students run. I don't have any agenda for them, so it's whatever they feel like talking about. That's turned out to be a useful way to run the courses to take care of this special problem that arose.

DB *In addition to your office being relatively neat and tidy, there are also some additions to the photography section on your wall.*

The latest photo has my three grandchildren sitting in a bathtub. I try to keep the other side of life, something to look at that's nice.

DB *There's a connection between my question and what I want to ask you about. There is much talk now of family values and children. You've been citing a UNICEF study by the economist Sylvia Ann Hewlett on Child Neglect in Rich Societies. What's that about?*

That's one of several interesting studies. That's the best. It came out in 1993. It has yet to be mentioned anywhere, as far as I know. UNICEF usually studies poor countries, but this is a study on rich countries and how they take care of children. She's a good, well-known American economist. She found, basically, in the last fifteen years, two different models. There's an Anglo-American model and a European/Japanese model. They're radically different. The Anglo-American model has been basically a war against children and families. The European/Japanese model has been supportive of families and children. And it shows. The statistics show it very well, as does experience. In Europe and Japan, family values have been maintained. Families have been supported. Children don't go hungry. Parents stay with children. There's bonding in early childhood because both husbands and wives are purposely given time to spend with children. There are day care centers. There's a whole support system. The U.S. and England, on the other hand, are basically at war with children and families and have destroyed them, purposely. Purposeful, conscious social policy has been to attack and destroy family values and children. So there are extremely high rates of child poverty and malnutrition, child abuse, parents and children having very little contact under the Anglo-American system. Contact time has fallen about forty percent over the past generation, in large part because two parents have to work 50-60 hours a week to survive, to keep the children alive. So you have latchkey children, television supervision, abuse of children by children, violence against children, etc. The amazing thing about the U.S., and this is an intriguing element of our intellectual culture, is that the people who are carrying out this war are able to say that they're defending family values and nobody cracks up in ridicule. That takes a really disciplined intellectual climate. The fact that nobody discusses it publicly—this is serious research, not the kind of junk that's called research—that's also revealing.

DB *I'm getting a signal from your office manager to wind this up. You've been citing some Hallmark cards that reflect these trends you've described. Where did you get them?*

I didn't. That's reported in the same study. As part of Sylvia Ann Hewlett's UNICEF study, the discussion of the breakdown of families under the conscious social policy of the Anglo-American system, she mentions as one sign of it this line of Hallmark cards, one of which is intended to be put under a child's breakfast cereal, saying, Have a nice day, because the parents are out somewhere. The other is to be tucked under the pillow at night, saying, Wish I were there. She gives that as an illustration of what's also shown by the heavy statistics. Incidentally, this is not the only such study. There is a bestseller in Canada by a woman who is a personal friend of mine, Linda McQuaig. She used to be a journalist and became a freelance writer. She's a very good social critic. She wrote a book (*The Wealthy Banker's Wife*) on the Canadian model. So it's Canada-focused. But she pointed out, rightly, that Canada is kind of poised between the Anglo-American model and the European model, moving toward the Anglo-American one. She describes in some detail what that's doing to families and children in a country that used to have a sort of civilized social contract. It's eroding under the pressure of the Anglo-American system that they're a part of. The book was a bestseller in Canada, but you're not going to find it around here. My own book, *Necessary Illusions*, was also a bestseller in Canada. It wasn't even reviewed here. There are other studies. And the facts are quite dramatic.

I notice you have a newspaper article.

DB *It's yesterday's* Denver Post. *Of course, the obligatory Superbowl coverage dominates the front page. But there's a story on a new study which reports that six million U.S. kids are poor and the numbers are increasing.*

Child poverty in the U.S. is just off the scale. Poverty altogether is. The U.S. has the most unequal distribution of wealth of any industrial country, and that's been radically increasing in recent years. Poverty among children is just awesome. In New York City it's about forty percent below the poverty line. New York City has as high a level of inequality as Guatemala, which has the worst record of any country for which there are data. People know what that means. Poverty among children is enormous. Malnutrition is unbelievably high and getting worse. The same is true of infant mortality. It's unique in the industrial world. And it's social policy.

Take, say, family leave. Most civilized countries nurture that. They want parents to be with children when they're little. That's when bonding takes place and a lot of child development takes place in those early months, even neural development. It's well known. So in a civilized country you try to provide for it. The U.S. does not even have the level of plantation workers in Uganda for these things. That's part of the war against children and families and in general against poor people that's carried out under the rubric of "family values." The idea is, only rich people should have state support. They have to be subsidized by massive transfer payments, like Newt Gingrich and his constituents. But poor people have to be smashed. Poor means most of the population. Incidentally, it's not only children who are suffering poverty, but also the elderly, surprisingly. There was a big article in the *Wall Street Journal* recently about how starvation, in their words, is "surging" among the elderly, reaching maybe 15 or 16% of the population over sixty. Again, that's a phenomenon unknown in industrial societies, and indeed, unknown in poor societies, because there they have support systems, extended families or whatever. But we're unusual. Civil society has been basically destroyed. Family structure has been devastated. There is a powerful nanny state, but it's a welfare state for the rich. That's an unusual system. And it comes from having a highly class-conscious business class and not much in the way of organized opposition.

DB *I'm afraid I'm going to be thrown out of here in an organized fashion. See you in a couple of days.*

***

February 3, 1995

DB *I want to impress upon our listeners about how competent and able we are. The other day we got off to a real Marx-like start, and I don't mean Karl. I forgot to turn the tape recorder on. Then when I did the phone rang and then you spilled your entire cup of coffee on the floor. It was a precious sequence.*

I'll avoid that now by cutting the phone connection.

DB *Just on a pile update, I see there has been some shifting of the piles. The left-hand pile has grown considerably.*

There's a Barsamian thermos mug on top of one of the piles, which helps.

DB *And the piles on the file cabinets behind you have grown significantly, just in a couple of days. Let's continue a little bit about Australia and what you found there. We did talk about East Timor, but in terms of the Australian economy, are they also part of the neoliberal paradigm?*

Australia is the only country in history, I think, that has decided to turn itself from a rich, First World country into an impoverished

Third World country. It is now unfortunately busily at work at it. Australia is in the grips of a fanatic ideology called "economic rationalism," which is a souped-up version of the free market theology that's taught in economics departments but that nobody in the business world believes for a second. It's the ideology which has been forced on the Third World, which is one of the reasons why it's such a wreck, but which rich countries have never accepted for themselves. They've always insisted on and demanded massive state intervention and protectionism, with the U.S. usually leading the pack, since 1800. You can see the differences. You go back to the eighteenth century and the First World and the Third World weren't all that different. They're rather different today, and this is one of the reasons.

Australia, which is in the Anglo-American orbit, and not a leading power, obviously, is a small country. They have taken the ideology seriously. They are doing what they call "liberalizing" their economy, meaning opening it up to foreign penetration and control, and to the main sources of capital in that area. East and Southeast Asia is a big growth area in the world. In fact, with one exception it's an enormous growth area. The one basket case is the Philippines, which has been enjoying our tutelage for a century. You're not supposed to notice that. But apart from that the area's in a big growth boom, in pretty awful ways, but nevertheless a growth boom. The source of it is mainly Japanese and overseas Chinese capital, which are two big imperial concentrations, although the overseas Chinese one is scattered. It's not territorially based. What they're trying to do is pretty clear. They want to turn Australia into their Caribbean. So they'll own the beach fronts and have the nice hotels and the Australians can serve the meals and there will be a lot of resources that they can pull out. Australia is still a rich country. In fact, at the time of the First World War it was the richest country in the world, so it has lots of advantages. It's not going to look like Jamaica very soon, but it's heading in that direction.

Since they dropped tariffs in this neoliberal fanaticism, the manufacturing deficit, meaning the ratio of manufacturing imports to exports has increased very sharply, meaning importing manufactures and exporting resources, services, tourism basically. It's moving in that direction. It's under very careful design, with a lot of smugness. Because the economists who studied at the University of Chicago and so on probably believe the stuff they were taught. Business leaders have never been willing to tolerate it for a second. But it is part of the ideological fanaticism that is part of the technique for smashing down poor people and sometimes rich people who take it on for themselves and suffer the consequences. The same thing happened in New Zealand.

DB *What was Australia's role in the U.S. attack on Indochina?*

Australian documents have been released up till the early 1960s and we now know that the Menzies government, the government of Australia in the early 1960s, was greatly afraid of Indonesia. That was their big concern. That concern still hasn't abated. They are on the edge of Asia. They regard themselves as a white outpost on the edge of Asia. There's always a yellow peril concern, very racist. It's being overcome now, I should say, but back then it was very racist. They felt that they had to switch. The British fleet used to be what protected them. But illusions about that collapsed during the Second World War, when the Japanese very quickly sank the British fleet. They realized that their protection was going to be the U.S., so they better be a subservient client to the U.S. As the U.S. moved into Indochina, they went along. They provided not a huge amount of aid—it's a small country—but they sent troops, so they carried out plenty of torture, atrocities, and so on.

They did this for two reasons. Part of it was just service to the big power, the big guys, who are supposed to protect them. But partly because they shared the U.S. geopolitical analysis, which was very straightforward, that there could be a demonstration effect of successful independent development in Indochina. They were worried about the same thing from China in those days. And that it could spread. It could, as they liked to put it, "infect the region." There could be an infection that could spread over the whole region. The way you get rid of an infection is you destroy the virus and you immunize those whom it might reach. And they did. They helped the U.S. destroy the virus.

The U.S. had basically won the Vietnam War by the early 1970s, as was clear to the business community. Nobody else seems to be able to understand it yet. In the region they simply supported the installation of extremely brutal, murderous regimes.

The most important was Indonesia, where there was a major event in 1965. The CIA pointed out in its report, which has since come out, that the slaughter that took place ranks right up with the Nazis and Stalin. They were very proud of it, of course, and said it was one of the most important events of the century. And it was. Indonesia was the rich area that they were afraid might be infected by the spread of independent nationalism. When the generals took over in the mid 1960s, General Suharto, in what the *Times* called admiringly a "staggering mass slaughter," destroyed the one political party in the country, the PKI, the party of the poor. Everyone agrees on this. The U.S. records, incidentally, have also come out through the 1950s at least, although they've been very secretive about them. They've been very selective about what they release. It's a little unusual. It's also been noticed by scholars. But there's enough there to know that what they were afraid of was that the PKI, the major political party, would win an election if there was ever an election. So therefore democracy had to be destroyed.

In the late 1950s, the U.S. carried out huge subversive operations designed to strip away the resource rich outer islands in a military uprising. That didn't work. The only alternative left was this "boiling bloodbath," as it was called in the press, which very much satisfied the U.S. There was total euphoria across the board. The same thing happened pretty much in Thailand and the Philippines and so on. So the region was inoculated. The virus was destroyed. Australia played a part in it. Since then they have been incorporated into what's called in the U.S. the "defense system," the military system. So that's their relationship to the U.S. But they have a separate relationship to Asia. That's the relationship of increasing subordination to Japanese and overseas Chinese capital that's quite visible. For example, of the three largest exporters, two are Japanese multinationals, which is the standard Third World pattern developing.

DB *Darwin, in his* Voyage of The Beagle *in 1839, wrote, "wherever the European has trod, death seems to pursue the aboriginal." How did the aborigines, the indigenous population of Australia fare? Did you have any contact with them while you were there?*

Some. In Tasmania they were simply totally exterminated. In Australia they were driven inland, which means desert. In the U.S., it's taken several hundred years. It's just two hundred years for Australia, they're a young country compared with us—they're beginning to recognize aboriginal rights, the land rights issue, etc. There is an independent aboriginal movement. Up till now there's been extreme racism, maybe worse than the American record. But it's changing, and now there are aboriginal rights groups. I was able to meet some of them. I was invited by the Timorese, and they're in contact with them. So there has been some legal recognition of aboriginal land rights and some limited rights to resources, but it will happen to the extent that the popular forces press it, as usual.

DB *There's been a noticeable shift in the emphasis of your public talks and your writing over the last decade. There's much more focus now on trade and economic issues. When did that occur? How did that come about?*

It came about from the 1970s, when the issues shifted. Some major events took place in the early 1970s, very significant. One of them was the breakdown of the Bretton Woods system, which we've talked about. That's one force that set in motion very substantial changes that gave a big acceleration to the growth of multinationals. Transnational corporations now have an enormous role in the world economy. These are just incredible private tyrannies. They make totalitarian states look mild by comparison.

The other huge change was the extraordinary growth in financial capital. First of all, it's exploded in scale. It's absolutely astronomical. There are close to a trillion dollars moving every day just in trading. Also the total composition of capital in international exchange has radically shifted. So in 1970, before the destruction of the Bretton Woods system, which meant regulated exchanges, about ninety percent of the capital in international exchanges was real economy related, related to investment and trade. Ten percent was speculative. By 1990 the figures were reversed. By 1994, the last report I saw was 95% speculative and it's probably gone up since. That has an extraordinary effect.

Its effects were noticed by James Tobin, the American Nobel Prize-winning economist, in his presidential address to the American Economic Association in 1978, so that's in the early stages. He pointed out that this rise of financial capital speculating against currencies is going to drive the world towards very low-growth, low-wage, and, though he didn't mention it, also high-profit economy. What financial capital wants is basically stable money. It doesn't want growth. This is why you see headlines in the papers saying, Federal Reserve Fears Growth, Fears Employment, we've got to cut down the growth rate and the employment rate. You have to make sure that Goldman, Sachs gets enough money on their bondholdings. He suggested at the time a tax on speculative capital, just to slow down the rate of capital exchanges. Of course that was never done. It's coming up in the U.N. It will be smashed, but it's still being discussed, simply to try to shift the balance towards productive investment instead of speculative and destructive interchanges.

Incidentally, it's had an enormous effect on the news business. The big wire services, like Reuters and AP, which is connected with Dow Jones, and Knight-Ridder, do give news, but that's a secondary function. The main thing that they do is interact instantaneously with financial markets. So if Clinton is giving a speech, the AP, Reuters, and Knight-Ridder reporters will be there, of course. If he says a phrase indicating maybe we're going to stimulate the economy, they race off with their mobile phones in their hands and call the central computer and say, Clinton said X. Then the guy who is manning the computer twenty-four hours a day types off to thousands of terminals around the world that Clinton said X, and maybe $700 million moves around in financial markets. The three wire services compete to make sure they get there first. I was told by a reporter who works for Reuters that every day they get a record of how they rank as compared with AP and Knight-Ridder, and it's in the microseconds. You've got to get there half a second before because there are huge amounts of money at stake. All this is destructive for the economy. It tends towards low growth, low wages, high profits. That's essentially what the wire services are about these days. Yes, there's news on the side, but that's slow stuff for us guys.

The telecommunications revolution, which expedited all of this, is, incidentally, another state component of the international economy that didn't develop through private capital, but through the public paying to destroy themselves, which is what it amounts to. This has been going on since the early 1970s, but it really hit big in the 1980s, primarily in the Anglo-American societies. So under the Reaganites and Thatcher, and with a spillover effect in Australia, New Zealand, and Canada (it's all one culture area). You get this development we talked about last time of the effects on families and children. That's just one effect.

DB *Where does the collapse of the Mexican economy factor into this?*

I just got a phone call a couple of days ago from a journalist in Mexico telling me that I'm a big figure there now because they had an interview with me in one of the Mexican journals (*La Jornada*, November 7, 1994) a couple of months ago in which I said this is all built on sand and is going to collapse. It was pretty obvious. It's what's called a Ponzi scheme. You borrow money. You use what you've borrowed to borrow more money, and finally the whole thing collapses because there's nothing behind it. Economists who know anything about Mexico didn't miss it. It's the ideological fanatics who didn't notice it, or claim not to.

The free market reform, so-called, "privatization," which everyone says is such a wonderful thing, means giving away public assets for a fraction of their worth to rich cronies of the president. Every president of Mexico, including Salinas, whom we're supposed to love, comes out a billionaire, for some reason, as do all of his friends and associates. The number of billionaires in the *Forbes* list of billionaires went up from one to twenty-four from 1989 to 1993 during the huge economic miracle.

Meanwhile the number of people below the poverty level increased at roughly the same rate. Wages have fallen about fifty percent. Part of the point of NAFTA was to undermine the Mexican economy by opening them up to much cheaper imports from the U.S. The U.S. has an advanced state-subsidized economy, so therefore you can produce things very cheaply. The idea was to wipe out middle-level Mexican business, keep the multinationals. There are Mexican-based multinationals. Keep the monopolies. Keep the billionaires. Lower wages. That's good for U.S. corporations. Then they can move over and get workers at a fraction of the wage. It's a very repressive state. You don't have to worry about unions and regulations. There has been a lot of capital flowing into Mexico, but it's well known that it was mostly speculative.

As far as the rich Mexicans are concerned, they just export their capital. They're not going to keep it there. So probably rich Mexicans lost very little from this devaluation. For one thing, they all knew it was coming because it's so totally corrupt that it was all known on the inside. If anyone looks, they'll find that Mexican capital probably went overseas very fast shortly before the devaluation.

So it's the American investors who are in trouble, big Wall Street firms. One Mexico specialist, Christopher Whalen, very conservative, who advises business, called the current Clinton plan a scheme to bail out Treasury Secretary Rubin and his friends. The Europeans know this. Just this morning the main European countries announced that they were going to back off from this. They don't see any particular point in bailing out rich Wall Street firms. But it's another one of those techniques by which you get the American taxpayer to pay off rich Americans.

This is essentially what happened to the debt crisis back in the early 1980s. Mexico had a huge debt. The debt was to U.S. banks, but they don't want to pay the cost. So it was basically socialized. When the debt is moved over to international funding institutions, as it's been, that means to the taxpayer. They don't get their money from nowhere. They get it from taxes. It's exactly what existing capitalism is about. Profit is privatized but costs are socialized. If Mexico wants to develop, it's going to have to do it the way every other country did, by not closing itself from international markets, but by focusing on domestic development, meaning building up its own resources, protecting them, maintaining them. It's got plenty. Not giving them away to outsiders. And they're going in exactly the opposite direction.

Part of this bailout is that Mexico is essentially mortgaging its one major resource, the oil reserves. The U.S. has been trying to get hold of those for forty years, and now we've got them. PEMEX, the big Mexican oil company, is probably completely broke. It looks good on statistics, but if any serious accountant took a look at it, they'd probably find that it doesn't have any capital. Because relative to other big oil companies it has been doing very little capital investment. That has a very simple meaning: you're not getting ready to produce for the future. But they do have the oil, and U.S. energy corporations would be delighted to take it over. Mexico is going down the tubes. That's what's called an economic miracle. It's not the only one. It's true of the hemisphere.

DB *It was really interesting to watch how this played out in the mainstream press. You've often talked about the needs of foreign countries to satisfy Wall Street investors. Rarely have I seen it so blatant as in this case. Mexico's finance minister goes to New York, makes a case and the*

Times *wrote, New York Investors Not Pleased With Him. He goes back to Mexico and gets fired. Then the new guy goes to New York, as did other finance ministers from Argentina and elsewhere, and the line was, New York Investors Take a Liking to Him.*

This one was so blatant you couldn't conceal it. It was all over the front pages. In fact, it was kind of interesting in Congress. The current Congress is not really a straight big business institution the way the Democratic Party usually is. It's got a mixture of very reactionary nationalist fanaticism. A large part of it is based on phony business, like yuppie-style business and some of it on the middle level, more nationalistic business. And they don't like it. They're not in favor of bailing out the big Wall Street firms. So you've had opposition from Congress and from people like Pat Buchanan and so on.

What's happened here is very interesting. If people weren't suffering, if you were looking at it from Mars, it would be interesting to watch. Big business for years has been trying to undermine and roll back the whole social contract, the welfare system, and so on. But there are elections. You can't approach the population and say, Look, vote for me, I want to kill you. That doesn't work. So what they've had to do is to try to organize people, as have other demagogues, on other issues, what they like to call "cultural issues." So what they've organized is Christian fundamentalists and jingoist fanatics and a whole range of extremists, plus plenty of people who live off the government but pretend that they're entrepreneurial, like the high tech culture, all publicly subsidized, but they pretend all sorts of entrepreneurial values. They're all big libertarians as long as the government's paying them off enough. Gingrich is the perfect example. So that collection of people is the only one they can mobilize. It's not hard in the U.S. It's a depoliticized society. There's no civil society. It's been destroyed. There is very deep fundamentalist fanaticism, widespread fear, a very frightened society, people hiding in terror. The jingoism is extraordinary. There's no other country that I know of outside the Soviet Union where you could have a concept like "anti-Americanism." Almost any country would laugh if you talked about that. But in the Soviet Union or the U.S. it's considered a totally normal thing. This is all a result of lots of corporate propaganda and other such things.

But the result is that they've now got a tiger by the tail. It's a little bit the way probably Hitler's backers in the industrial-financial world felt by the late 1930s. The only way they were able to organize people was in terms of fear and hatred and jingoism and subordination to power. Pretty soon they had these maniacs running around taking political control of the state. The state is a powerful institution. We're getting something like that in the U.S. There is an anti-big business mood among the troops that big business has mobilized. The reason is they couldn't mobilize them on any other grounds. You couldn't mobilize them on the real project, namely kill yourselves. That won't work. So they had to do it around other projects, and there aren't a lot around. So you get something like—I don't want to draw the analogy too tightly, because things are different—it has something of the feel of Hitler Germany and Khomeini Iran, in which similar sorts of things took place. The business sectors in Iran, the merchants, the *bazaaris*, the guys who wanted to get rid of the Shah, they did organize Islamic fundamentalists. And they weren't happy with the results. Something similar is happening here.

DB *Is that the major internal problem that you see for the rollback crusade?*

I don't know how big a problem it is. The point is that the concentration of private capital is by now so extraordinary and so transnational in scale that there isn't much that can be done in political systems to affect it. The London *Economist* had a great phrase that captures it. They were describing the elections in Poland, where the Poles, not understanding how wonderful their economy is, voted back the old communists into power. About half the population of Poland said they were way better off when they were under communism. We know it's an economic miracle. They don't understand it. The *Economist* assured its readers that it didn't really matter, because, as they put it, "policy is insulated from politics." So in other words, these guys can play their games, but there's enough private tyranny to ensure what the World Bank calls "technocratic insulation." You keep doing the same things no matter what these guys say at the ballot box.

Probably that's true. If you look at the programs that are being pushed through now in the U.S., they're very carefully crafted to protect the rich. The New York budget that came out yesterday was a very good example. It's worth taking a close look at. They say they're lowering taxes, but it's a total lie. For example, if you lower state support of mass transportation, that has one immediate consequence, namely costs of riding public transportation go up. And that's a tax, a very carefully crafted tax, not on guys who ride around in limousines but on working people. So in fact they will cut income taxes. In that sense, taxes are being cut. But the tax system is getting less progressive. They'll cut taxes. But meanwhile they'll increase taxes for the poor, the people who have to ride the subway. Elderly people who are at home and can't get out and need shopping services, that's going to be cut, which means the costs are transferred to the poor. They're not yet going after Medicare, because rich people get Medicare. But they went after Medicaid, which goes to poor people. Cut mental health services. The rich will get them anyway. If you look at the budget carefully, it's a very carefully honed class warfare designed to crush the poor even more. I don't mean welfare mothers. I mean working people. I'm talking about eighty percent of the population. Smash the poor more. Enrich the rich. Inequality at the level of Guatemala isn't good enough. They want to make it more extreme. That's the so-called populism, the fight for the middle classes. Those are the policies that are getting rammed through.

DB *A couple of months ago Labor Secretary Robert Reich said, If you're going to talk about welfare, let's talk about "corporate welfare." How far did that idea go?*

He gave a talk which was well reported in the foreign financial press. The London *Financial Times* had a big report on it. It was mentioned around here. It was shot down instantly by the White House. They told him right away to shut up. The *Wall Street Journal* had a nice article about it a couple of weeks later, a good article, in which they reported about the enormous subsidies being given to corporations under the new Gingrich program, which they said was going to make boardrooms delighted. In the course of the article they said, Well, Robert Reich did make this speech about ending corporate welfare as we know it, but he was instantly shot out of the water by the White House. It was made very clear that no such plans were on the agenda. Quite the opposite. We're working for you guys, don't worry about it. But it's a term that's in the public eye at the moment, although as yet very little mentioned in the U.S., and instantly silenced by the Clinton White House.

DB *Robert Siegel is the co-host of National Public Radio's* All Things Considered. *In an exchange he had with Jerry Markatos, a colleague of mine, in North Carolina, Siegel says that "attacking welfare for the rich is a staple of mainstream Democratic rhetoric. Chomsky's observation about this is not exactly cutting edge stuff."*

Of course, I've been talking about it for years, as have others out of the mainstream. He may believe what he said. He probably doesn't know anything about the facts. These guys are just supposed to read the words that somebody puts in front of their face. The fact is that "attacking welfare for the rich" was shot down instantly. It's not a Democratic staple. In fact, the Democrats made it extremely clear and explicit that they weren't going to let this go anywhere. Reich was called on the carpet for it. Siegel may simply not be aware of the facts, which is very likely. And incidentally, the point that Markatos raised had nothing to do with what is sometimes called "corporate welfare," but rather something different and far more important: the Pentagon-based system of public subsidy for high technology industry. Apparently Siegel missed the point completely, again, not too surprising since these topics are not likely to be discussed in his circles.

DB *But Siegel doesn't leave it at that. Markatos asked him, Why don't you have Chomsky on NPR once in a while? He said he wasn't particularly interested in hearing from you and that you "evidently enjoy a small, avid, and largely academic audience who seem to be persuaded that the tangible world of politics is all the result of delusion, false consciousness, and media manipulation."*

He knows as much about that as he does about the staples of Democratic political discourse. Actually, I did have a discussion with him once, which was kind of interesting. A book of mine called *Necessary Illusions*, which was on the media mainly, was based on invited lectures given over Canadian national public radio. It was then published and was in fact a bestseller in Toronto. I never saw a review here, as far as I recall. But there was a fair amount of public pressure on NPR. On *All Things Considered* they have an authors interview segment. So under various kinds of pressure they finally agreed to let me have one of those five-minute interviews. It was with Siegel.

I didn't listen. But it was announced at 5:00 that it was going to be on the next half-hour segment. People listened. It got to 5:25 and it hadn't been on. Then there were five minutes of music. At that point people started calling the stations, saying, What happened? They didn't know what happened, so they started calling Washington. The producer of the program said it had played. She said it was on her list and it played. People asked her to check. It turned out it hadn't played. She called me. I didn't pay any attention one way or the other. She was kind of apologetic. Somewhere between 5:05, when it was announced, and 5:25, when it was supposed to go on, it had been canceled by somebody high up. She said that the reason was that they thought Robert Siegel's questions weren't pointed enough. If true, the fact that anyone even checked at that point shows how terrified the NPR liberals are that some doctrinally unacceptable thought be expressed. She asked me would I do it again. So I said sure. It's a pain in the neck going down to the station. But I went down again. He tried to ask pointed questions. You can draw your own conclusions. That they did run. That's our one interchange.

As to the audience, there's some truth to it. It's true that there are some countries, the U.S. is one, the others are mostly Eastern Europe and other totalitarian systems, where I have had almost no access to the major media over the years. That's not true elsewhere. First of all, there are plenty of audiences in the U.S. I don't have any problem talking with the people I'd like to talk to. In fact, I can't do a fraction of it. They're students, popular groups, churches, etc. But the thread of truth beneath what he says is that in the U.S., as in Russia, the major media may have been very sure to exclude not just me, but anybody with a dissident voice.

You showed me the Markatos-Siegel exchange (*Current*, January 16, 1995) right after I came back from Australia. There I gave a talk at the National Press Club, which was nationally televised (twice), at the Parliament Building, I was not talking about the U.S. They wanted me to talk about Australia's foreign policy. So I talked about Australian foreign policy to journalists, parliamentarians, officials, and a national audience. I was not very polite, but very critical, because I think the foreign policy is disgraceful. I was on their world services program beamed to Asia. I was interviewed on that for about half an hour on the Timor Gap Treaty, a very important matter. All over the press and the papers. The same is true elsewhere. I have articles and interviews in major journals up and down the hemisphere, and many invitations from leading journals that I unfortunately have no time to accept; I'd like to. I just had an article in Israel's most important daily journal, an invited critique of their foreign policy. They don't want me to talk about the U.S. They wanted a critique of the so-called peace process. The same is true in Europe. So as far as Robert Siegel is concerned, there are two possibilities. Either he understands something about me that, outside the Soviet Union, no one else knows. That's one possibility. There's another possibility, that he resembles the commisars in a different way. People can make their own decision.

DB *Let's turn to one of our favorite topics, which is of course sports. There is a major labor action going on that a lot of people know about, and that's the baseball strike. Have you been following that?*

No, I'm afraid not.

DB *There's an interesting component to this which I think you should know about. The owners are demanding that their workers, the players, put a cap on their earnings. But no similar cap is being asked to be put on the owners' ability to make profits.*

That sounds like the norm. I'll bet you without looking at it that most of the population is blaming the players. I suspect, it's just the way media and corporate propaganda usually works.

DB *That just played out here in Massachusetts. Governor Weld wants to give money to the owner of the New England Patriots to spruce up the stadium and build luxury boxes and improve road infrastructure and the like. There was a poll in yesterday's* Boston Globe *that most of the people want it. They think it's a good idea. That's not welfare.*

No, because it goes to rich people. This is part, again, it's a matter of people paying for their own subordination. Maybe it's fun to watch baseball games. In fact, I like it, too. But the fact of the matter is that the way this stuff functions in the society is to marginalize the people. It's kind of like gladiatorial contests in Rome. The idea is to try to get the great beast to pay attention to something else and not what we powerful and privileged people are doing to them. That's what all the hoopla is basically about, I would guess.

DB *Decatur, Illinois, is the site of three major labor actions. The corporations involved are Staley, a British-owned company; Bridgestone, which is the number one tire and rubber maker in the world and is Japanese-owned; and Caterpillar, the number one producer in the world of earth-moving equipment. At Staley there's a lockout. At Bridgestone and Caterpillar the workers are on strike. The* New York Times *is calling this a "testing field in labor relations" and also saying that "in Decatur more than anyplace else labor is trying to halt its slide toward irrelevance."*

There is a whole long story here. The U.S. has an extremely violent labor history, unusual in the industrial world. Workers here didn't get the rights they had in Europe until the mid-1930s. They had had those rights half a century before in Europe, even in reactionary countries. In fact, the right-wing British press, let's say, the London *Times*, couldn't believe the way U.S. workers were treated. Then finally the U.S. workers did get some rights. It caused total hysteria in the business community. They thought they had the whole country by the throat, and they learned that they didn't.

They immediately started a counterattack. It was on hold during the war but took off right afterwards, with huge campaigns. There was a nice phrase that one of the corporate leaders used. He said there is "an everlasting battle for the minds of men" and we have to win it. They put billions of dollars into this. In the early 1950s, when all this stuff took off, business-made movies were reaching twenty million people a week. It was a huge campaign. They had what they called "economic education programs" to teach people what we want the truth to be. They forced workers in plants to go to them. It was called "released time." They had to go to these courses. There were millions of pamphlets distributed. About one-third of the material in schools was produced by the business communities. Churches and universities were also targeted for subversion. Even sport leagues were taken over. The huge entertainment industry was enlisted in the cause. For business, it was a deadly serious matter. The anti-communist crusade was tied up with this. That's its true meaning. It was a way of using fear and jingoist sentiments to try to undermine labor rights and functioning democracy.

The labor bureaucrats played their own role in this. Business was worried at the time. By the end of the Second World War the U.S. population had joined the general social democratic currents sweeping the world. Almost half the work force thought that they'd do better if the government owned factories than if private enterprise did. The unions in the late 1940s were calling for worker rights to look at the books and intervene in management decisions and to control plants; in other words, to try to democratize the system, which is a horrifying idea to pure totalitarians like business leaders. So there was a real struggle going on. It worked through the 1950s, largely driven by anti-communism. During the 1980s the unions were really crushed.

There was a series of Caterpillar strikes. The first one was critical, because it was the first time the government endorsed the hiring of what they called "permanent replacement workers," in other words, scabs in manufacturing industry. The U.S. was condemned by the International Labor Organization for that, which was extremely unusual. The ILO is a very conservative organization and they don't offend their big funders. But they did call on the U.S. to adhere to international labor standards. Maybe Robert Siegel reported it on NPR. That was a major event. This is the next stage.

They now feel, because of these developments in the international economy, business tastes blood, they think they can roll back the whole social contract that's been developed over the past century through popular struggle: labor rights, human rights, the rights of children to have food, anything other than making profit tomorrow.

It's important to remember that we don't have a capitalist economy, because such a thing couldn't survive, but it's quasi-capitalist, so there are market forces and competition. In such a system you're driven to very short-term goals. Part of the nature of that kind of system is you can't plan very far. You want to make profit tomorrow. If you don't show a good bottom line tomorrow, you're out and somebody else is in. The result is they destroy themselves. That's one of the reasons why business called for government regulation a century ago, when they were playing around with *laissez-faire*. They quickly saw that it was going to destroy everything. So much of the regulatory apparatus was put in under business control.

But now they're more fanatic and they want to destroy the regulatory apparatus. It's clear what that's going to mean. The timing was almost delicious. Last December, when the Republicans were announcing their moves to try to eliminate and demolish the regulatory apparatus by a variety of methods, which is what they're planning to do, right at that time there was a series of reports that came out about some of the effects of having done this in the 1980s. One of the most striking was right here in New England: Georges Bank, which has been the richest fishing area in the world. They had to close a lot of it down. Now New England is importing cod from Norway, which is like Australia importing kangaroos from Turkey. The reason they're doing it is that Norway preserved its fishing grounds. They have a different "philosophy," as they put it here. Our philosophy is to rob everything as much as possible and forget about tomorrow. Their philosophy is to consider the needs of the population, now and in the future. What happened is that the government combined subsidies to the fishing industry with deregulation. You know what that's going to mean. You pay off people to deplete fish resources and you don't regulate what they do and they deplete them. In fact, they've depleted ground fish. Whether they will recover or not nobody really knows. Scientists don't know enough about it. But maybe they've destroyed the richest fishing area in the world forever, or maybe somehow it will be able to recover.

This came out at the same time that they were announcing further cutbacks in regulation. Then along comes the Mexican collapse. It's another example. Deregulate everything, enrich the rich, which is what privatization is, and you can see what's going to happen. And if something goes wrong, turn to the public for a bail-out, because "capitalism" requires privatizing profit but socializing cost and risk. Incidentally, in the same weeks, NASA came out with new satellite data announcing the best evidence yet, for a rise in sea level, which means the effect of global warming. They also announced in the same satellite data, that they traced the effect of the depletion of the ozone layer to industrial chemicals. That comes out at the same time that they're saying, Let's cut back the last residue of regulatory apparatus. But it makes a certain sense if the sole human value is making as much wealth as you can tomorrow. You don't care what happens down the road and you don't care what happens to anybody else. It makes perfect sense. If it destroys the world, well, it's not my problem.

DB *We hear these horns and things in the background. Is this office over a railroad track?*

It's actually a change from the way it once was. When I got here in the 1950s it was an industrial area. The industrial plants have been wiped out. The working-class living areas have been leveled. But at that time we were between a leather factory, a tire-burning factory, a chocolate factory, and a soap factory. Depending on which way the wind was blowing, you had a nice combination of odors. Now it's mostly government-supported high tech small industries.

There are very few trains around. The reason is that the U.S. government carried out probably the biggest social engineering project in history in the 1950s, pouring huge amounts of money into destroying the public transportation system in favor of cars and airplanes, because that's what benefits big industry. It started with a corporate conspiracy to buy up and eliminate street railways and so on. The whole project suburbanized the country and changed it enormously. That's why you got shopping malls out in the suburbs and wreckage in the inner cities. It was a huge state social engineering project.

It's continuing. For example, a couple of years ago, Congress passed the Transportation Subsidy Act to give the states money to support transportation. It was intended to maintain public transportation and also to fill potholes in the roads. But the figures just came out, in the same month of December, and it showed something like ninety-six percent of it went to private transportation and virtually nothing to public transportation. That's the point of getting things down to the state level. Big corporations can play around with governments these days, but state governments they can control far more easily. They can play one state against another much more easily than one country against another. That's the purpose of what they call "devolution," let's get things down to the people, the states. Corporations can really kick them in the face, and nobody has a chance. So the idea will be that you get block grants that go to the states, no federal control, meaning no democratic control. It will go precisely to the powerful interests. We know who they are: the construction business, the automobile corporations, and so on. Meaning whatever there is of public transportation is very likely to decline.

Yesterday's New York budget is a striking example. It doesn't say it, but it implies increasing the fares for public transportation and decreasing service, while making sure that the guys in the limousines are doing quite fine.

So you hear a couple of freight trains in the background, but unless they can be shown to serve private power, they're not going to be around long. Incidentally, one of my favorite remarks in diplomatic history is in a great book on Brazil by a leading diplomatic historian, also senior historian of the CIA, who describes with enormous pride how we took over Brazil in 1945 (Gerald Haines, *The Americanization of Brazil*). We were going to make it "a testing area" for "scientific methods" of development in accordance with capitalism. We gave them all the advice. He's very proud of this total wreckage, but who cares? Brazil had been a European colony, so their railroad system was based on the European model, which works. Part of the advice was to switch it over to the American model. If anybody has ever taken a train in pre-Thatcher England or France and then in the U.S. they know what that means. But he said this with a straight face. Another part of their advice was to destroy the Amazon.

DB *When you were in Chicago in October, a woman in the audience asked you, in a pretty straight-ahead question, how come you don't factor gender into your analysis? You pretty much agreed with her, but you really didn't answer her question.*

In fact, I've been writing about it quite a bit in recent books in connection with structural adjustment, globalization of production, and imposition of industrialized export-oriented agriculture. In all cases, women are the worst victims. Also in some of these latest articles. What we discussed the other day about the effect on families is essentially gender war. The very fact that women's work is not considered work is an ideological attack. As I pointed out, it's somewhere between lunacy and idiocy. The whole welfare "debate," as it's called, is based on the assumption that raising children isn't work. It's not like speculating on stock markets. That's real work. So if a woman is taking care of a kid, she's not doing anything. Domestic work altogether is not considered work because women do it. That gives an extraordinary distortion to the nature of the economy. It amounts to transfer payments from working women, from women altogether and working women in particular, to others. They don't get social security for raising a child. You do get social security for other things. The same with every other benefit. I maybe haven't written as much about such matters as I should have, probably not. But it's a major phenomenon, very dramatic now.

Take these latest New York welfare plans again, or the ones they're thinking about in Congress. One of the things they're going to do is to force women under twenty-one, if they want to get welfare, to live with their families. Take a look at those women. A substantial percentage of them have children as a result of either rape or abuse within the family. These advocates of family values say either you send your kid to a state orphanage or you live with a family which may be an abusive family and may be the source of your problems. But you can't set off on your own and raise children, because that's not work. That's not a life. You have to get into the labor market.

All of this is a major phenomenon in contemporary American affairs and in fact in the history of capitalism. Part of the reason why capitalism looks successful is it's always had a lot of slave labor, half the population. What women are doing isn't counted.

DB *I've never heard you, for example, use the term "patriarchy." While not wanting to hold you to the fire with particular terms, is it a concept that you're comfortable with?*

I don't know if I use the term, but I certainly use the concept. If I'm asked about what I mean by anarchism, I always point out that what it means is an effort to undermine any form of illegitimate authority, whether it's in the home or between men and women or parents and children or corporations and workers or the state and its people. It's all forms of authority that have to justify themselves and almost never can. But it's true. I haven't emphasized it.

DB *Are there any books by feminists that you read and value?*

I sort of read it. What I read I sort of know, so I'm not learning anything. Maybe other people are. It's worth doing. I think it's had a very positive effect on the general culture. But unless you call things like Hewlett's UNICEF study of child care feminist literature—which I wouldn't, I'd just call it straight analysis—no, I don't know it very well.

DB *Russia has been a great success story. The military attacked the Parliament and it managed to win that battle, but what about the awesome display of Russian military might in the Chechen republic?*

My view has long been that the Cold War was in large part an aspect of the North-South conflict, unique in scale but similar in its basic logic. With its end, it is therefore not surprising to find that Russia is largely returning to the Third World where it belonged and where it had been for half a millennium. Right after 1989 not only Russia but most of Eastern Europe goes into free fall, returns to Third World conditions. The old Communist Party is doing fine. They're happier than they ever were. They're richer than they ever were. Inequality has grown enormously. The leadership is mostly the old *nomenklatura*, the guys the West always liked and want to do business with now.

UNICEF just did a study just on the human effects of the so-called reforms, which they approve of, incidentally. They estimated that in Russia alone there were about half a million extra deaths a year by 1993 as a result of the reforms that we're so proud of. That's a fair degree of killing, even by twentieth-century standards. The same leadership is in control. Take Yeltsin, for example, whom the West favors. He's a tough old party boss and knows how to kick people in the face. There's the rise of a huge mafia, like every other Third World country we take over, starting from southern Italy in 1943, but in fact all through the world, there's a major mafia.

Incidentally, Mexico, too. In Mexico under the economic miracle the government is increasingly linked up with cocaine cartels. Jeffrey Sachs made his fame, this guy who goes around telling countries how to save themselves, by the economic miracle in Bolivia. But what's usually only pointed out in the footnotes is that Bolivia stabilized its currency all right, but mostly by shifting to cocaine exports, which is perfectly rational under the advice that he gave them of becoming an agro exporter. It's happening in the former U.S.S.R., too. Huge mafia, spreading to the U.S. because there are plenty of immigrants here. Selling off resources. In Kazakhstan there are a lot of resources and there are American businessmen all over the place trying to buy up the oil. If a country that's that well-behaved wants to carry out massacres, the U.S. isn't going to object. The U.S. hasn't tried to prevent the Chechnya massacres, any more than it did Saddam Hussein's gassing of Kurds.

DB *Here I am with this barrage of questions partly written out. I'm dealing with a loaded deck and you're just sitting there. It's like Russian* *roulette, in a way. You don't know what's coming next. Are there ever any moments where you're thinking, He's really missing the point. Why doesn't he ask that?*

Your questions are so perfect, how could I think that?

DB *You're impossible! Any sense of maybe cutting down on your public speaking schedule?*

Actually, I have to cut down a bit this spring because I have some extra teaching. I've doubled the teaching that I usually have. But not in general. I have to think about what I'm going to do for the next couple of years anyway. Retirement age isn't that far away. But I've had too much to do to think about the future.

DB *In all these talks that you've given, you must have reached hundreds of thousands of people, your articles, the interviews, the radio, the TV. It must put a tremendous, not just a physical burden on you, but an emotional one, too. Everything is riding on your shoulders. I'm concerned about that, just as a friend.*

I don't feel that way at all. I feel I'm riding on other people's shoulders. When I go to give a talk in Chicago, say, I just show up. They did all the work. All I did is take a plane, give a couple talks, and go home. The people there did all the work. I just came back from Australia. Those guys have been working for months to set everything up, and they're still working. I went, had a nice time, talked at a bunch of places. I'm exploiting other people. Actually, it's mutual exploitation. I'm not trying to be modest about it. There are some things that I can do pretty well. Over the years I've tried my hand at a lot of things.

DB *Like what?*

I did spend a lot of time, believe it or not, organizing and going to meetings, like in the early days of Resist, of which I was one of the founders. I religiously went to all the meetings and sat there and was useless and bored. Finally, out of all this a kind of division of labor emerged by mutual consent. We would all do the things we can do. There are some things I just can't do at all and other things I can do very easily. I do the things I can do easily. But the serious work is always done by organizers. There's no question about that. They're down there every day, doing the hard work, preparing the ground, bringing out the effects. There is absolutely no effect in giving a talk. It's like water under a bridge, unless people do something with it. If it is a technique, a device for getting people to think and bringing them together and getting them to do something, fine, then it was worth it. Otherwise it was a waste of time, self-indulgence.

DB *Speaking of resistance, what forces can resist the right-wing onslaught?*

An overwhelming majority of the population is very strongly opposed to everything that's going on. The question is, can they be successfully diverted and dissolved and separated from one another? We talk about having to teach lessons in democracy to Haiti. Anyone with a grey cell in their head would laugh and collapse in ridicule at that. We have to learn lessons in democracy *from* Haiti. Here's a country in miserable conditions, worse than anything we can imagine, with a population that was able on their own effort to construct a lively, vibrant, functioning civil society with unions and grassroots organizations and, without any resources, to sweep their own president into power and create an actual democratic society. Of course, it was smashed by force, with us behind it. Nobody's going to smash us by force. But if we could learn the lessons of democracy from Haitian peasants, we could overcome these problems.

DB *Why don't we end here and maybe you can make some headway on these piles.*

OK. *(Chuckles)*

History and Memory

May 9 and 12, 1995

DB *Here you are—I want you to be the first kid on your block to have the new Nixon stamp. Speaks volumes for American political culture.*

The nicest comment I've ever gotten in the *New York Times* was from William Safire about Nixon, remember that?

DB *No.*

I had written an article in the *New York Review* about Watergate. I said I thought it was sort of a tea party and didn't mean a thing and compared it with COINTELPRO, which came out at the same time. I said, Look, if you want to talk about something really serious, talk about that. But Watergate was just marginal. So William Safire picked it up and had a column about it, saying, Finally somebody told the truth about it. Then I started getting letters from little old ladies in Ohio saying, Thank you for defending our President. It was unusual praise from the *New York Times*.

DB *I want to talk to you about history and memory and, if you'll excuse the expression, how they're constructed. The Czech writer Milan Kundera has written, "The struggle of man against power is the struggle of memory against forgetting." In the context of all of these anniversaries that have been coming upon us in waves, from D-day to V-E Day, there's one in particular that I'd like you to talk about. August 6th marks the fiftieth anniversary of the bombing of Hiroshima. I guess you were sixteen at the time. Where were you when you heard the news?*

I was actually a counselor at a summer camp up in the Poconos when the news came through by radio, I guess. We probably didn't have any newspapers. I was pretty shocked by it. I took off by myself for a couple of hours and walked in the woods and just thought about it. I came back and never talked to anyone because nobody seemed to care. So it was just a sort of personal reaction.

But I must say that Nagasaki strikes me as much worse. Nobody's done much research into Nagasaki, so I can only speculate, but my impression is that the Nagasaki bomb was basically an experiment. Somebody ought to check this out, I'm not certain, but I think that they basically wanted to discover whether a different mechanism was going to work and used a city because, I don't know why, why not a city? If that turns out to be true, even five percent true, it's the most grotesque event in history, probably. Certainly the most grotesque scientific experiment in history.

Whatever you think about Hiroshima, maybe you can give an argument, maybe you can't (I don't really think you can) but at least it's not in outer space. I can't conceive of any argument for Nagasaki. And then it doesn't stop there, of course. There was that event which I wrote about thirty years ago which I never see mentioned, although it's in the official Air Force history. It's what the official Air Force history calls the "finale." General Hap Arnold, who was Air Force commander, decided that to end the war it would be nice to do it with a bang, with a kind of grand finale. What he wanted to do was to see if he could organize a thousand planes for a raid on Japan. Getting a thousand planes together was a big managerial achievement in those days, sort of Schwarzkopf-style. But he managed to get a thousand planes, and they bombed cities, civilian targets, on August 14. This is described in a very upbeat description in the Air Force history. It was after the surrender had been announced but before it had been officially received. Then when you move over to the Japanese side, there was Makoto Oda, a well-known Japanese novelist who was maybe fourteen or fifteen at the time, living in Osaka. He wrote an article which describes his experiences. He remembers the August 14th raid and he claims that with the bombs they were dropping leaflets saying, Japan has surrendered. That one didn't kill as many people as the atom bombs, but in a way it's more depraved.

In fact, speaking of memories, March 10th was a memory. It was the fiftieth anniversary of the bombing of Tokyo. That passed here without a whisper. If you look at the U.S. Strategic Bombing Survey after the war, it points out that more people were killed during that bombing in a six-hour period than ever in human history. The bombing of Tokyo virtually leveled the city. It was mostly wood, so therefore they started by dropping oil gel, which sets things on fire, then napalm, which was then just coming in. According to survivors, the planes were just chasing people. There was no defense. It was a defenseless city. They used napalm to block the river so people couldn't get to it. People did try to jump into ponds, but then they just burned to death because the ponds were boiling. I don't know what the total was. It's estimated somewhere between 80,000 and 200,000, which puts it very much on the scale of the atom bombs, maybe bigger. They so totally destroyed Tokyo that it was taken off the atom bomb target list because it would have had no effect other than piling rubble on rubble and bodies on bodies, so it wouldn't have shown anything. It's just astonishing.

The *Far Eastern Economic Review*, which is a right-wing journal run by Dow Jones, publisher also of the *Wall Street Journal*, commemorated it with a detailed article and a picture of what Tokyo looked like after the firebombing. It's unbelievable. There are two or three buildings standing. The rest is just flat.

DB *Do you recall what it was about Hiroshima that caused you so much consternation? Were you aware of the implications?*

The implications were pretty obvious. Even the little bit of information that came across was that one plane had flown across to an undefended city and dropped one bomb, which they then described and the number of people they had killed. But it was obviously monstrous. That does open a new era, no question. It means the destruction of the world is well within reach, quite apart from the nature of this attack. I had had various amounts of skepticism about the war right from the beginning. The war against Germany was one thing. But this part was quite different, in my opinion. Growing up in that period, you just couldn't miss what John Dower wrote about recently. The treatment of the Germans and the Japanese was radically different. If you go back and look at war films—these are childhood memories, I can't be certain—but my memories are the Germans, who were by far worse in everything they did, incomparably worse, were treated with some respect. They were blond Aryan types, whereas the Japanese were vermin to be crushed. Plus all the story of the sneak attack and the day that would live in infamy and so on, you can't take that seriously, and I didn't at the time. Bombing Pearl Harbor and Manila is doubtless a crime, but by the standards of the twentieth century, even by then, it's just invisible. They bombed military bases in colonies that had been stolen from their inhabitants, in the

Philippines by killing a couple hundred thousand people, and in the case of Hawaii by guile and deceit and treachery. To bomb military bases in colonies that had been stolen from the inhabitants no doubt is a crime, but pretty low down on the scale.

Incidentally, there are plenty of Japanese atrocities. Japan had carried out horrifying atrocities, but that didn't cause all that much of a reaction. Nobody cared much.

In fact, right up to the end, there were negotiations going on between Japan and the U.S., Cordell Hull, the Secretary of State, and Admiral Nomura, right up till Pearl Harbor, I think until a week before the bombing. The main issue of contention was that the U.S. insisted that the Asian system be an open one, meaning everybody had a right to participate freely. So the U.S. had to maintain its rights in China. Japan at the end finally agreed to that, but they insisted that this be worldwide so that the Western Hemisphere would be open. Cordell Hull, who was a terrible racist, considered this outrageous, as did other American commentators.

This picks up a theme that goes way back through the 1930s. The Japanese from the beginning, from the time they began to expand, this particular phase of expansion, had said that they were trying to create in Asia something comparable to the Monroe Doctrine. That touched a nerve in the U.S., because there was more than a little truth to that. And there were all kinds of efforts through the 1930s to distinguish the Monroe Doctrine from the Japanese new order in Asia. They're worth reading. I reviewed them in an article ("The Revolutionary Pacifism of A.J. Muste: On the Backgrounds of the Pacific War") about thirty years ago. They are amazing to read, up till the end. They end up by saying, How can they dare make this comparison? When we exert our power in the Caribbean and the Philippines it's for the benefit of people. It's to improve them and uplift them and help them, whereas when the Japanese do it, it's aggression and atrocities.

If you look closely, one of the things I wrote about—I was just rereading that article, wondering whether to reprint it, there's a lot of new scholarship, but as far as I know it changes nothing—was to review recently released Rand Corporation studies of Japanese counterinsurgency documents in Manchuria. They had carried out a campaign in Manchuria and they described it in some detail and the Rand

Corporation released it. They're quite fascinating reading. It was very close to what the U.S. was doing in Vietnam at the same time. They professed no interest in any gain for Japan. The Kwantung Army, which was running it, had a kind of social democratic rhetoric, in a sense. They wanted to create an earthly paradise for the people of Asia, wanted to save the people of Manchuria, what they called Manchukuo, like we called our client state South Vietnam. They wanted to save the people of Manchukuo from Chinese bandits and fascists and communists (the Russians were right there) and give them a chance to develop independently in cooperation with Japan. The same in China, where they established a puppet regime, but under the control of a well-known Chinese nationalist, certainly with all the credentials of the people we were supporting in South Vietnam. And full of love for the people and high ideals and anti-communism. I just compared it point by point with what Dean Rusk and other people were saying about Vietnam at the time. Aside from a stylistic difference, it wasn't very different. It translated very closely.

It's kind of interesting. This article of mine has occasionally been mentioned in the U.S., and it's regarded as an exculpation of Japan. It's regarded as justifying the Japanese, comparing them to what we were doing in Vietnam, which tells you something about the American psyche. If you compare something to the horrifying atrocities that the U.S. was conducting in Vietnam, then that shows that you're an apologist for them. How can anybody criticize us? What we're doing must be magnificent.

Which raises another slight memory. We also just passed the twentieth anniversary of the departure of U.S. troops from Vietnam. It was interesting to see how that passed. Unfortunately, it's just a broken record, so I don't even have to repeat it. But the complete incapacity of anyone in the spectrum here, across the spectrum, of seeing that there was anything more involved than a failed endeavor, that's pretty amazing. It happened to coincide with McNamara's memoirs. That's a story, too.

DB *I want to talk to you about* McNamara *in just a second. But was that article in* American Power and the New Mandarins?

It was reprinted there. It was originally in *Liberation*, the anarchist journal. A.J. Muste had just died, and Nat Hentoff was putting together a volume of essays for him. A.J. Muste was a revolutionary pacifist. The framework of the article was, Let's test his thesis in the hardest case, when the country is attacked. Technically the country wasn't attacked, but let's say the U.S. was attacked. In that case, does it make sense to be a pacifist? He was. He thought we should not fight that war. Then I said, How can we evaluate that position? I went on in some detail into the background of these things.

The background is quite interesting. August 6th will be coming along, and there is going to be endless discussion about the war in Asia. We'll just look and see what is said. For example, what is going to be said about the comparison to the Monroe Doctrine? What's going to be said about the fact that the U.S. was pretty supportive of Japan right through the 1930s? As late as 1939, Ambassador Grew, who was the leading specialist on Japan, was defending the Japanese conquest in China. In fact, the big debate then was, Are they going to cut off our access to China? What is going to be said about the 1932 Ottawa Conference, where Britain, at that point unable to compete with much more efficient, not cheaper labor, but more efficient Japanese production, simply abandoned the laissez-faire doctrine, free trade, which they had instituted when they figured they were going to win the game because they were richer than anyone else? They couldn't compete any longer, so they abandoned it and closed off the Empire. For a country like Japan, without resources, dependent on trade, for the British to close off the Empire, meaning at that time India, Australia, New Zealand, Borneo, Malaya—it was not technically closed off but they raised tariffs so high that Japan couldn't get in. The Dutch did the same in the East Indies, what's now Indonesia. The U.S. did the same. We were a much smaller power then, but in the Philippines and Cuba, that was closed off, in effect. And here is Japan saying, We're latecomers in the game, admittedly, but we want to play the game the same way you guys do. If you block trade, we'll just have to use force, the same way you did in the first place. They specifically compared it with the Monroe Doctrine. You can have any view you like about this, but to discuss the Second World War without discussing these things doesn't even reach the level of idiocy. So we'll know in a couple of months how much of this was discussed. I think we can make a pretty fair guess.

DB *It's amazing to see how fifty years later Hiroshima is still such a* *contentious issue. Recently there was a huge ado about the Smithsonian's Air and Space Museum exhibit on the atomic bombing. Subsequently the director resigned under fire from Congressmen and veterans' groups and other monitors of history. What is it that makes this such a passionate issue?*

I was involved in that. As you know, I'm a neurotic letter writer. I'm one of those people who signed that statement of historians saying, This ought to be opened up to discussion. It can't just be closed. It said, Maybe the exhibit has to be criticized, but let's have a serious exhibit and look at the history. The Smithsonian backed off from that under pressure from the American Legion and some veterans' groups and so on and political pressure, including by the *Washington Post*, which went berserk over this issue. How dare you raise this question? Any question that might indicate that we're not perfect and they're not devils? My favorite article is by Charles Krauthammer. I hate to quote from memory, but my recollection is that he said something about how what we should have is the *Enola Gay* and it should be an object of reverence. In other words, we should pray to this idol and revere it because it succeeded in massacring people, and since that's our job, we should not only accept it but revere it, like a god. That's the extreme.

After I signed that statement, there were about fifteen hundred people who signed it, I started getting letters from outraged people. I wouldn't be surprised if I was the only person who ever answered the letters. But I did answer them, because I'm always intrigued. And besides, I feel you ought to answer letters. So I answered them and got into some interesting correspondence, which varied. At one point a piece of one of my letters was published in some Air Force journal, with a violent diatribe about these anti-American fanatics. The letters ranged. There were people with whom I had a perfectly serious correspondence, for example, veterans who said, I was out there at the time and I just wanted to get home alive and I didn't care what they did. Okay, that's understandable. I don't agree, but we're sort of in the same moral universe.

But others were insane. There were people who sent me articles written saying, History should be nothing more than a record of data. You should show the *Enola Gay*, you should show August 6, period. Anything that goes beyond data is political correctness taking over. Of course, they don't believe that of anything else, but on this one they do. And basically the theme was, We've got to worship the *Enola Gay*. There is a history here, too. For years—I don't know if it's still true—at air shows, the regular Texas air shows, every year the pilot of the *Enola Gay* would fly a replica of it and thousands of people would cheer. There aren't many countries that celebrate atrocities like that.

It was rather intriguing to compare. The anniversary of the fire-bombing of Tokyo was on March 10th. That was about three weeks after the fiftieth anniversary of the bombing of Dresden, which was mid-February some time. The bombing of Dresden was pretty bad. Nobody knows, but I think numbers like maybe 30,000 or 40,000 people killed are used. They destroyed a civilian city. They originally thought it was a military target, but they apparently knew in advance that it wasn't. That was the British and the American Air Forces, under British command. The British press had quite a lot of soul-searching about this. I haven't seen anything here. Britain was under attack at that time. That's when V-2 rockets were coming. Britain had, first of all, suffered, was threatened, and was still under attack. They didn't know until the last minute how that war was going to end. If the Germans had been a little bit more advanced with jet planes and V-2 rockets it could have gone their way. The U.S. was never attacked. I think a couple of balloons flew over Oregon or something, but the British are able to reconsider whether the destruction of Dresden was legitimate, and we can't. Because we are perfect. We are holy. We revere our murderers because they are gods, and the more people they kill the more godly they are. That's our history. One example is Theodore Roosevelt's *Winning the West*, which ought to be read by every student in every college. It's just proto-Nazi.

DB *Getting back to Hiroshima again, there are just a couple more things I want to touch on with you about that. You've heard the traditional rationalizations for it. I'm sure they're going to be repeated* ad nauseam *in August. The bombing was a military necessity. Had the U.S. invaded there would have been one million casualties.*

I don't think any serious historian even takes that seriously at all any more. One can argue about whether it was worth doing or not. It's not an open-and-shut case. On the other hand, there is pretty strong evidence now that they never considered anything like that level of casualties. That's a number that Truman threw around once in his diary, but the actual numbers estimated (Barton Bernstein at Stanford has probably done the most detailed work on this from the documentary record) are, I think, about 50,000 or 60,000. Aside from that, there's no reason to believe there ever would have been an invasion. The invasion was planned for November, and another one for the next May or some months afterwards. But there was pretty good reason to think that Japan would have surrendered by then. In fact, again, the Strategic Bombing Survey said that Japan couldn't have held out that long, atom bombing or not.

Quite apart from that, there's a question about the legitimacy of an invasion. Why did we have to occupy Japan? Maybe it was right, maybe it was wrong, but it's not obvious. For example, the fact that Japan had attacked two military bases in two U.S. colonies hardly gives us a justification for occupying it. Of course, Japan had carried out plenty of atrocities. But we didn't care about the worst ones in the 1930s. We paid very little attention. There was some criticism, some embargoes, this and that. But they were mostly not because of the atrocities. During the war Japan carried out tons of atrocities. The Bataan Death March, the treatment of prisoners, and so on. But that's in the context of the war, and we weren't too pretty either if you look at what was happening. So there is a question about the invasion of Japan. You can give an argument for that, too, even from the Japanese side. There were plenty of Japanese who, I think, wanted that invasion. It's a complicated story.

One thing that the invasion did was it restored the imperial system. MacArthur and the Americans purposely covered up Emperor Hirohito's crucial role in the war and the atrocities because they wanted to keep the imperial system as a way of controlling Japan. And they did cover it up. It's a pretty horrible story.

But nevertheless, the invasion did undermine to some extent the legitimacy of the imperial system. Therefore it created an opening for Japanese democrats that they wouldn't have had otherwise. So that's a factor. You can debate that. I should say that the net effect of the invasion is a complicated story. Overall, it probably undermined Japanese fascism and left some kind of opening for Japanese democracy. On the other hand, it was a very mixed bag.

By 1947, the U.S. had undertaken what it called the "reverse course," which meant in effect restoring the old fascist structures, the *zaibatsu*, the conglomerates. They smashed up the labor unions, pretty much what the U.S. did around the world. It started in Japan around 1947. George Kennan was once again instrumental in that reversal, a nice record all across the board. But it's a mixed story. If you want to look at the invasion, there are many facets, including the question, Why invade? But if it was agreed that we should have invaded, there is strong reason to believe that the invasion would have been just an occupation of a country that had surrendered, atom bomb or not.

Aside from that, there's the question of the Russians. The Russians came in, I think, around August 8. That was a terrible blow to the Japanese. They could not withstand a Russian land invasion, and they knew it. It's very likely that a large part of the motive in the atom bombing was to cut off the possibility of Russian participation in control over East Asia. The U.S. took a very strong line on that. We not only kept the Russians out, we kept the British and the French and the Dutch and everyone out. The Far Eastern Commission, which was supposed to oversee Japanese affairs, the U.S. ruled with an iron hand. They wouldn't let anyone in. Kind of like the Monroe Doctrine. In the Middle East at least the U.S. let the British in. But in Japan, nothing. There are good studies of this. So this is going to be our show. And certainly not the Russians. You can debate exactly the extent to which the atom bomb was motivated by those considerations, but it was certainly not trivial.

DB *I was talking to Michio Kaku some weeks ago. He told me a really interesting story. His parents were interned, as were tens of thousands of Japanese-Americans. He said that the motive behind the internment had to do with the rich agricultural lands that the Japanese farmers had, particularly in California, and that these were confiscated by the government and then handed over to agribusiness. Have you heard that?*

I've heard that. I've never researched it, so I can't say, but I've certainly heard it. I think that was the outcome. How much it was the motive I don't know.

DB *I come from the Upper East Side of New York. There were a lot of Germans there. The Bund was marching around in the 1930s, in fact, right up until the war, but one didn't hear any calls for internment of German-Americans.*

I was in Philadelphia in a German and Irish Catholic neighborhood. We were the only Jewish family there. The neighborhood was very anti-Semitic and pro-Nazi. I remember beer parties when Paris fell, and it lasted up until December 7, 1941. In fact some of my dramatic childhood memories are watching the guys who were cheering for the Nazis one day come around with little tin hats and telling everybody to pull down their shades the next day, a very sudden transition. But there was no internment of Germans. It's not that they were treated nicely. The German POWs were sent to re-education camps, as were the Italians, which was completely illegal. The U.S. had to keep it secret because they were afraid the Germans would retaliate with the U.S. prisoners. So they were renamed. At first they were called re-education camps. Then they were called some other fake name. The idea was to brainwash them, what's called "teaching them democracy." They were kept in the U.S. until about mid-1946. They were used for forced labor. Some were killed. They were kept in England several years later. Did you know Peggy Duff? She was the main person in the international peace movement for years. Her first activity was exposing the British re-education camps for German and Italian prisoners. We actually know a lot about the German side of it, because the Germans keep very good records. The Italians, nobody knows a thing. They were probably treated much worse, because they didn't keep any records. But you're absolutely right, there were no German-Americans interned.

DB *Michio told me another thing in terms of duration. Some Japanese-Americans, including his parents, were kept in the internment camps almost a year after the war ended. There was compensation much later, after many of the people had died. Again with this issue, the question of memory: Politicians and pundits today often cite World War II and that era as not only just the good war, but there were no moral ambiguities. Right was right. Wrong was wrong. Americans were united. There was great cooperation. People were making sacrifices. Is that how you remember it?*

There is a lot of truth to that. During the war there was tremendous unity. People were making, not sacrifices of the kind that the Russians made, but you weren't driving as much as you used to, and you wouldn't buy a new refrigerator, those kinds of sacrifices. And of course American soldiers fought.

But there were plenty of moral ambiguities. The moral ambiguities went before and started during the war again. So the U.S. and Britain were very pro-Mussolini. Even after the invasion of Ethiopia the U.S. accelerated its sale of oil to Italy in violation of the embargo. Italy was loved. Mussolini was that "admirable Italian gentleman," as Roosevelt called him. After the March on Rome in 1922 and the establishment of Italian fascism and the smashing of the Parliament, the destruction of the trade unions, the torture chambers, and so on, American investment boomed. Mussolini was very much admired across the board, including by the left, I should say. In the 1930s U.S. investment shifted mostly to Germany. Germany became after Britain the leading recipient of U.S. investment. There were very close relations between German and American firms. American firms were participating in the Aryanization program, the robbery of Jewish properties. The U.S. government, the State Department, for example, was taking quite a favorable attitude toward the Nazis at least until 1937. The line was that Hitler was a moderate and we have to support him because he's standing between the extremes of left and right and unless we support him there will be a rise of the masses. The British were even more favorable to Hitler. Lord Halifax went to Germany in 1937 or 1938 and told Hitler how much the British admired him. This continued almost until the war. Then, as soon as the war got started, the first thing the U.S. and Britain did as they started liberating the Continent was restoring the fascist structures, very openly.

DB *Christopher Hitchens had a brilliant essay, in a recent* Monthly Review, *on Munich. It's always talked of as "appeasement." He said it wasn't appeasement. It was collaboration.*

I wrote him a letter after that mentioning to him some additional documentation. It was as you say an excellent essay, but the truth is even worse than he says. The documents are very explicit. They say, We must support Hitler. It's the same kind of thing they say about every Third World gangster they support these days. It's the only barrier against the masses, who will otherwise rise up and take away everything from the people of property. So of course we have to support Hitler. This goes right through to 1937 and 1938. The same was going on in Spain. Basically the U.S. and Britain were kind of supporting Franco. They didn't openly support him, but the policies that they adopted were pretty much pro-Franco. For example, there was an embargo, but Franco was getting everything except oil. That's the one problem he had. He managed to get oil. How? From Texaco Oil Co., which happened to be run by an open Nazi. The Texaco Oil Co. had contracts with the Republic. It broke them. The ships that were out at sea were rediverted to Franco. This continued right through the war. The State Department always claimed it couldn't find it, didn't know anything about it. I even read it at the time. The little left-wing press could find it. They were reporting it. But the State Department couldn't find it. Later of course they conceded that it was happening. Meanwhile, some American businessman tried to send pistols from Mexico to the Republic. Roosevelt gave a press conference in which he bitterly denounced him. He said, Of course it's not technically illegal, but some people just have no patriotism at all. On the other hand, Texaco selling oil to Franco was just fine. We just had a repeat of that in Haiti, which the press is still sitting on. Texaco also sent oil to the Cédras junta with the agreement of the Bush and Clinton administrations.

DB *Let's keep on this theme of history and memory. Robert McNamara is perhaps the epitome of "the best and the brightest". He has the number one bestseller in the country today:* In Retrospect. *He writes, "We of the Kennedy and Johnson administrations who participated in the decisions on Vietnam acted according to what we thought were the principles and traditions of this nation. We made our decisions in light of those values. Yet we were wrong, terribly wrong. We owe it to future generations to explain why. I truly believe that we made an error not of values and intentions, but of judgment and capabilities."*

Actually, he's correct about the values. If somebody tries to disobey us, our values are that they have to be crushed and massacred. Those are our values. They go back hundreds of years, and those are exactly the values that they acted upon. His belief that it was a mistake—personally I agree with the hawks on this. He's been criticized by the doves who say, You came around too late, and by the hawks who say, Well, it was a victory. And the hawks are right. It was a victory. So it wasn't a mistake. He doesn't understand that. He doesn't understand very much, incidentally. The one interesting aspect of the book is how little he understood about what was going on or understands today. He doesn't even understand what he was involved in.

I assume he's telling the truth. The book has a kind of ring of honesty about it. What it reads like is an extremely narrow technocrat, a small-time engineer who was given a particular job to do and just tried to do that job efficiently, didn't understand anything that was going on, including what he himself was doing.

But you're right. There's only one criticism that he sees, or that any of his critics see, or even his supporters, the whole range of discussion, including people who were very active in the peace movement, I should say. I've been shocked by this, the people who are active in the peace movement who are saying, We're vindicated because he finally recognized that we were right. It was an unwinnable war.

What about the maybe, if you count them up, four million Indochinese that died, something on that order. What about them? Actually, he has a sentence or two about them, and even that sentence is interesting. He talks about the North Vietnamese who were killed. An interesting fact about the book—and you can't blame him for this, because he's just adopting the conventions of the culture that he comes from, he's completely uncritical and couldn't think of questioning it—throughout the book the "South Vietnamese" are the collaborators whom we installed and supported. He recognizes that the population was mostly on the other side, but they're not "South Vietnamese." The attack on them doesn't appear.

The most interesting part of the book, in my opinion, the first thing I looked at when I read it, is what he would say about the two major decisions that he was involved in. He was involved in two basic decisions. He implemented orders, of course. One was in November and December 1961, when the internal resistance was overthrowing the U.S. client regime after it had already killed probably 80,000 people, eliciting internal resistance which Washington's terror state couldn't withstand. Kennedy just turned from straight terror, which it had been before, to outright aggression. They unleashed the American air force against Vietnamese villagers, authorized napalm, started crop destruction. They also started attacks against the North, which was not involved seriously at the time. That was the first big decision. He doesn't even mention it. I don't think he's concealing anything. I don't think he thought of it as a decision. Because after all, we're just slaughtering South Vietnamese, and that doesn't harm us at all. So why shouldn't we do it? Nobody's going to get angry. Nobody's going to harm us if we kill South Vietnamese. So when we send U.S. planes to napalm Vietnamese villages, what could be the problem? So that's not even mentioned.

The second one is even more interesting. In January 1965 they made the decision to escalate radically the bombing of South Vietnam. They also started bombing North Vietnam at the time, February 1965. But the bombing of South Vietnam was tripled in scale, and much more devastating. That was known. In fact, one person who describes that right at the time—and this is a very interesting aspect of McNamara's book and of the commentary on it—was Bernard Fall, a French military historian and Indochina specialist. A big hawk, incidentally. It's "we" and "them." He was on "our side" and that sort of thing. But he happened to have a missing gene or something. He cared about the people of Vietnam, although he was a hawk and a military historian who supported the French and then the Americans. He didn't want to see the place destroyed. In 1965, he wrote that the biggest decision of the war was not the bombing of North Vietnam, not the sending of American troops a couple of months later, but the decision to bomb South Vietnam at a far greater scale than anything else and to smash the place to bits. He had also pointed out in the preceding couple of years that the U.S. had been destroying the so-called Viet Cong with napalm and vomiting gases and massive bombardment and it was a massacre. He said in 1965 they escalated it to a much higher attack, and that was a big change. He was an American advisor. He describes how he flew with the American planes when they napalmed villages, destroyed hospitals. He described it very graphically. He was infuriated about it, but he describes it.

McNamara refers to those articles. He says, Fall's reports were "encouraging" and justified the U.S. escalation. McNamara didn't mention the decision to vastly increase the bombing of South Vietnam. That's just passed over. Nor is there discussion of the bombing of South Vietnam in general. He just passes over it without comment. He cites Fall's articles and says, Part of the reason that we were encouraged to proceed was that Fall was a fine analyst and knowledgeable person and was very impressed with what we were doing and thought it was going to work. There's a certain truth to that. Fall was saying, Yes, these guys are such murderous maniacs that they may succeed in destroying the country. In that sense, he thought it was going to work.

Then McNamara has a footnote in his book. He says two years later, Fall had changed his mind about the efficacy of American actions and took a more pessimistic view about the prospects for American victory. That was 1967. Look at what he wrote in 1967. He said this just before he died. He said Vietnam is literally dying under the worst attack that any country has ever suffered and it was very likely that Vietnam as a cultural and historical entity was going to become extinct under the American attack. And McNamara reads this and says he changed his mind about the efficacy of what we were doing. Not only did he write that, but every reviewer read it. Nobody comments on it. Nobody sees anything funny about it. Because if we want to destroy a country and extinguish it as a cultural and historical entity, who could object? Fall was talking about South Vietnam, notice, not North Vietnam. The killing was mostly in South Vietnam. The attack was mostly against South Vietnam.

In fact, there's an interesting aspect of the *Pentagon Papers*, too. The *Pentagon Papers* were not very revealing, contrary to what people say. I had advance access to them, since I had been helping Dan Ellsberg in releasing them, so I wrote about them in a lot of detail and very fast because I had already read them. But one of the very few interesting things about the *Pentagon Papers* which I wrote about at the time was the disparity between the planning for the bombing of the North and the planning for the bombing of the South. On the bombing of the North, there was meticulous, detailed planning. How far should we go? At what rate? What targets? The bombing of the South, at three times the rate and with far more vicious consequences, was unplanned. There's no discussion about it. Why? Very simple. The bombing of the North might cause us problems. When we started bombing the North, we were bombing, for example, Chinese railroads, which happened to go right through North Vietnam. We were going to hit Russian ships, as they did. And there could be a reaction somewhere in the world which might harm us. So therefore that you have to plan for. But massacring people in South Vietnam, nothing. B-52 bombing of the Mekong Delta, one of the most densely populated areas in the world, destroying hospitals and dams, nobody's going to bother us about that. So that doesn't require any planning or evaluation.

Not only is it interesting that this happened, but also interesting is the fact that no one noticed it. I wrote about it, but I have yet to find any commentator, scholar, or anyone else, who noticed this fact about the *Pentagon Papers*. And you see that in the contemporary discussion. We were "defending" South Vietnam, namely the country that we were destroying. The very fact McNamara can say that and quote Bernard Fall, who was the most knowledgeable person, who was utterly infuriated and outraged over this assault against South Vietnam, even though he was a hawk, who thought Saigon ought to rule the whole country—you can quote him and not see that that's what he's saying—that reveals a degree of moral blindness, not just in McNamara, but in the whole culture, that surpasses comment.

DB *Just a couple more things on McNamara and his mea culpa. He's sort of taken the Nazi Nuremberg defense, following orders, allegiance to the Führer, that's why he didn't speak out while he was Secretary of Defense.*

I don't agree. He does not recognize that anything wrong was done. So there's no question of a defense.

DB *On* MacNeil-Lehrer, *he now says he had misgivings about the policies.*

What were the misgivings? The misgivings were that it might not succeed. Suppose that some Nazi general came around after Stalingrad and said, I realized after Stalingrad it was a mistake to fight a two-front war, but I did it anyway. That's not the Nuremberg defense. That's not even recognizing that a crime was committed. You've got to recognize that a crime was committed before you give a defense. McNamara can't perceive that. Furthermore, I don't say that as a criticism of McNamara. He is a dull, narrow technocrat who questioned nothing. He simply accepted the framework of beliefs of the people around him and that's their framework. That's the Kennedy liberals. We cannot commit a crime. It's a contradiction in terms. Anything we do is by necessity not only right, but noble. Therefore there can't be a crime.

If you look at his mea culpa, he's apologizing to the American people. He sent American soldiers to fight an unwinnable war, which he thought early on was unwinnable. The cost was to the U.S. It tore the country apart. It left people disillusioned and skeptical of the government. That's the cost. Yes, there were those 3 million or more Vietnamese who got killed. The Cambodians and Laotians are totally missing from his story. There were a million or so of them. There's no apology to them.

It's dramatic to see how this is paired once again—I've been writing about this for years—with discussions of the inability of the Japanese to give a fully adequate apology for what they did during the Second World War. The Prime Minister of Japan has just been in China, where he apologized profusely for the atrocities that Japan carried out and the suffering of the people of Asia caused by Japanese aggression. That's been discussed in the *New York Times*, critically. Because, well, yeah, sure, he said it, but there are some Japanese parliamentarians who think he shouldn't have said it, so that the Japanese are still unwilling to face up to what they did. Next column over, we're facing up to the fact that we harmed the U.S. by destroying three countries and killing millions of people. It's pretty interesting. I don't think any country in history could have exhibited this shocking force on the front page without comment. Incidentally, there's no comment in the whole West. It's not just the U.S. In the British and the European press, to the extent I read it, it's exactly the same. This is part of Western culture. It's what Adam Smith called the "savage injustice of the Europeans," which already in his day was destroying much of the world.

DB *Long before McNamara wrote this book you had compared him to Lenin. What did you mean by that?*

I compared some passages of articles of his in the late 1960s, speeches, on management and the necessity of management, how a well-managed society controlled from above was the ultimate in freedom. The reason is if you have really good management and everything's under control and people are told what to do, under those conditions, he said, man can maximize his potential. I just compared that with standard Leninist views on vanguard parties, which are about the same. About the only difference is that McNamara brought God in, and I suppose Lenin didn't bring God in. He brought Marx in.

DB *The* Times *the day before yesterday had a front-page story:*

"The Radical Right Has an Unlikely Soulmate In the Leftist Politics of the Sixties." It states: "There is a sense that the Vietnam era war turmoil tore a hole in the post-World War II social fabric and that although it was the left that opened the rift, it was the right that has driven a truck through it." What do you think the newspaper of record has in mind in comparing the sixties with what's happening in the nineties?

That makes perfect sense from their point of view. Since everything the U.S. does is by necessity correct, except maybe it fails, or maybe it costs us too much, but otherwise it is by necessity correct, therefore the Vietnam War was of necessity correct and legitimate, except maybe for its failures, and the left was criticizing and therefore opened up this rift.

I doubt if *Pravda* would have gotten to this level, but maybe it would have. Suppose you had read *Pravda* about the invasion of Afghanistan, which was criticized. They say, You've got these critics, like Sakharov and these people, who are tearing a hole in the body politic by undermining Russian authority by saying we shouldn't defend the people of Afghanistan from terror. I suppose you can imagine that appearing in *Pravda*. I don't know for certain that it did. If so, *Pravda* would have descended to the level of the *New York Times*, which sees it exactly that way. They saw it that way at the time, as did the leading doves, who questioned the war because of its apparent failures and its costs, primarily its costs to us. By those standards, no one had a right to criticize the Soviet invasion of Czechoslovakia: it worked, and casualties were very few. Virtually no one in the main stream was capable of even imagining the position that everyone took in the case of Czechoslovakia: aggression is wrong, even if it succeeds and at a small cost. The criticisms were so tepid they were embarrassing. Almost nobody, including me, dared to criticize the U.S. attack on South Vietnam. That's like talking Hittite. Nobody even understood the words. They still don't. But from their point of view it's true. Actions taken to try to stop a murderous aggressive war that was massacring people and destroying three countries—that's tearing wide the body politic, and now the right can drive a truck through it. So, yes, that's the picture.

DB *You usually have the last word, but I'm going to say something here at the end. I want to just read you this quote. "During these last three* *decades, all my thoughts and actions in my entire life have been moved solely by the love and fidelity I feel for my people. This has given me the strength to make the most difficult of decisions, the like of which no mortal has ever made before." Have a sense of where that comes from?*

Himmler?

DB *It's Hitler.*

***

May 12, 1995

DB *I'm going to pick up the thread from the other day. We talked about history and memory. I just want to get a little closure to that. In general, who are the gatekeepers of history?*

Historians, of course. The educated classes in general. Part of their task is to shape our picture of the past in a way which is supportive of power interests in the present. If they don't do that, they probably will get marginalized in one way or another.

DB *How about some suggestions for people in terms of decoding and deciphering the propaganda? Are there any kinds of practical techniques? It's a tough question.*

I actually think it's a simple question. Use your common sense. You can point to examples. When you read a headline in the *Wall Street Journal* that says "American Oil Companies Fear Loss of Jobs in the Middle East," it doesn't take a genius to figure out that "jobs" is being used to mean "profits." When you read the account of the New York tax system which says they're cutting down subsidies to mass transit, you can quickly understand that subsidies means gifts from people to themselves. What they're doing is increasing taxes. You can go on and on, case by case. But there's no trick other than just using your sense.

DB *Can you recommend some basic books for people?*

There are things that are helpful, like Howard Zinn's *People's*

History, for example. It's a good start to give you a picture of the world that's different from the one you learned at school. It's very accurate. And then it's on from there. I hate to give suggestions. You just have to do what's called "triangulating." You try to look at the world from different perspectives. You're getting one perspective drilled into your head all the time, so you don't need any more of that one. But look at other ones. There are others. There are independent journals, dissident scholarly literature, all sorts of things. One of the reasons I give rich footnotes is to answer that question, because a lot of people want to know. There are things I think are instructive, but you have to decide for yourself what's interesting for you.

DB *Jumping into the present and the political climate, you have likened it to Germany and Iran. What do you mean by that?*

I was referring to a specific phenomenon that's becoming visible. How important it is is not entirely clear. But if you look at Germany in the late 1930s, or Iran around 1980, which is what I was talking about, there were big centers of power. In Germany it was the big industrialists. In Iran it was the *bazaaris*, the merchant class. They had an enemy in both cases. In the case of the big industrialists in Germany, it was the working class. They wanted to destroy the working class organizations. In the case of Iran, it was the Shah. They had helped in the organization of popular forces to overcome their enemies. In Germany it was the Nazi party. In Iran it was the fundamentalists. Then they both discovered something. The guys they had organized had ideas of their own, as did their leaders, and they weren't necessarily their ideas. So by the late 1930s, a lot of German industrialists were quite worried that they had a tiger by the tail in the case of Hitler. In Iran, they just lost. The fundamentalists took over and booted them out.

If you look at the U.S. now, the Fortune 500, the real big business, they are just euphoric. Social policy has been designed to enrich them beyond their wildest dreams. The annual issue of *Fortune* devoted to the Fortune 500, which just came out this week, reports profits up 54% over last year on barely rising sales and virtually flat employment. This is the fourth straight year of double-digit profit growth, which is just unheard of. They expect it to continue. So they're euphoric. They like a lot of this stuff. Most of what's going on in

Congress they just love. It's all putting money in their pockets and smashing everyone else.

But they're also worried. They can read the headlines, which tell them that these Gingrich freshmen congressmen are anti-big business, which is true. They don't like big business. They like what they call "small business," which is not so small. The big plutocrats are what they don't like, because they don't distinguish them from big bureaucrats. A lot of their policies are of a kind which real corporate power is not very happy about. In part that's true of what they call the "cultural scene." The only way they could mobilize their troops—you can't organize people if you say, Join me, I'm going to smash you in the face. So the way you do it is say, Join me, and because you can hate your neighbor, put black teenagers in jail, or you'll have religion, you organize people on the basis of fanaticism and extremism and hysteria and fear and then those people have their own ideas. There's no question that there is a lot of concern about this. You can see it again in places like *Fortune* magazine.

DB *Let's look at just some of the rhetoric today. These are quotes: "jackbooted government thugs," "The final war has begun," "Death to the new world order," "feminazis," and "environmental wackos." People like G. Gordon Liddy on his radio talk show are advising listeners on how to kill federal agents: "Head shots, head shots, ... kill the sons of bitches." And Newt Gingrich saying that Democrats are "the enemy of normal Americans."*

That's the kind of talk that does trouble the CEOs. George Bush wrote a very angry letter resigning from the NRA for that kind of reason. He's an old-fashioned sort of Eisenhower Republican, a corporate flack, and he doesn't think they should be going around talking about killing federal agents. But more important than that, these people are worried. Right now Newt Gingrich can say anything he likes about Democrats as long as he maintains funding for the Pentagon, which is the big cash cow for a large part of corporate America, including Newt Gingrich. But you can never tell when it's going to get out of hand. And I suppose Newt Gingrich is worried that it's going to get out of hand. He's enough of a slave to big business to worry about the fact that the guys that he's organizing can go off half-cocked from his point of view.

There's an interesting story about that in this morning's *Globe*. Take a look at it before you leave. They have a columnist called David Shribman, who's their rising hotshot. He just won a Pulitzer Prize. He's their political columnist now, to the left-liberal side by American standards. He has an article about Newt Gingrich. He says, We liberals have been misunderstanding him. He's not anti-government the way these fruitcakes are. He is in favor of government. But he wants government to do the right thing. So he wants government to be around to give laptop computers to the poor and all sorts of nice stuff. He just doesn't want a lot of crazy bureaucrats hampering initiatives. So he's really on our side. He quotes Michael Kazin, a left writer, saying that Gingrich is our kind of guy, a populist. He says that Gingrich is in favor of independence and entrepreneurial values and wants the government to stimulate that. The only thing he doesn't mention is that Gingrich insists that the government fund private enterprise. He himself represents Cobb County, which gets more federal subsidies than all but two suburban counties in the U.S. That's not mentioned. The reason is the class interest of suppressing the role of the government in funneling funds from the poor to the rich. That has to be suppressed, even at the left-liberal side. But meanwhile they do recognize that Gingrich is more committed to rational corporate power than a lot of the people that he's organized, who are dangerous and who could destroy things that they care about.

DB *Anthony Lewis, today or yesterday in the* Times, *got it wrong, though. He said that Cobb County in Georgia receives more federal funding than any other county in the country.*

That's incorrect. But finally they're sort of noticing. However, what's interesting is that this is suppression of the fact. To be able to suppress this all this time is astonishing. The suppression reflects the class interests. What Shribman's article indicates is that they recognize that they want to support what they see as a Gingrich-style Republicanism, which will indeed rely on huge state power to fund the rich, but not destroy the instruments of that power.

DB *Getting back to history and memory and the consequences of vitriolic speech, there was some notice of the Kent State killings after twenty-five years. Incidentally, no mention of Jackson State, in* Mississippi, *where* *two African-Americans were killed. If you recall the atmosphere, Nixon calling students "bums" and the Governor of Ohio, James Rhodes, the day before the shootings at Kent State, said, "We are going to eradicate the problem. These people just move from one campus to another and paralyze the community. They are worse than brownshirts, and also they're worse than the night riders and vigilantes." The next day were the killings.*

That's true, and I'd worry about the kind of quotes you talk about, but I think that that's barely the icing on the cake. The quadrennial analysis of public attitudes by the Chicago Council on Foreign Relations just came out. Among other things, they investigate what people think is the most serious problem facing the country. By a long shot, it's crime. Where did that come from? What does crime mean? And drugs are way high up. The OECD just did a study of drug money, about half a trillion dollars profit a year, they estimate. Over half of that passes through U.S. banks. Is that what they're talking about? Is that the crime and drugs people worry about? No. It's like you say, the black teenager. Has that kind of crime gone up? No, as far as we can tell. In fact, most of what they're calling crime is a kid caught with a joint in his pocket. Why do people think of that as the problem? That's not because of Rush Limbaugh. That's because of the mainstream commentary, which has stimulated fear of crime and shaped it in a very special sense to mean those superfluous people out there who are the wrong color and have the wrong genes. That's what you've got to be afraid of. That's a lot more important than Rush Limbaugh saying "feminazis."

DB *Conspiracy theories are nothing new in American history. Richard Hofstadter has written about* The Paranoid style in American Politics. *But there seems to me to be a difference now in terms of the instruments of purveying these theories. They have media. They have radio. People listen to it.*

That's true, but I still feel that I'm more worried about the *New York Times* and the *Boston Globe* than I am about Rush Limbaugh. So I think that with all the crazed lunacy about black helicopters, the U.N., and the Council on Foreign Relations, it doesn't begin to have the damaging effect of the way they shape public perceptions on issues like crime or like alleged free-market programs or welfare. That's far more dangerous. For example, Americans feel that they're being overtaxed to pay black mothers. In fact, our welfare system is miserly. It's gone down very sharply in the last twenty years. We're undertaxed. Those are things that really matter.

DB *In* Language and Responsibility, *in a discussion about FBI COINTELPRO operations and Watergate, you say that "one of the keys to the whole thing (is that) everyone is led to think that what he knows represents a local exception. But the overall pattern remains hidden." Is there a subtext to the Oklahoma City bombing there?*

I'm not sure exactly what you had in mind. In what sense?

DB *What's going on underneath?*

The U.S. wants to be able to carry out Oklahoma City bombings in other countries, as we do, but they don't want them to happen here. You're not supposed to blow up federal buildings here. That's something we do, not something that's done to us. Sure, they don't like that. But as for subtext, they don't like the fact that paramilitaries are out of control, that's for sure. There have been fifty years of propaganda stimulating anti-government feeling. Here's where I again don't care so much about Rush Limbaugh as I do about the mainstream. There have been fifty years of propaganda which suppresses the fact that the government reflects powerful, private interests, and they're the real source of power.

So take the angry white males who are maybe joining what they mistakenly call militias, paramilitary forces. These people are angry. Most of them are high school graduates. They're people whose incomes have dropped maybe 20% over the last fifteen years or so. They can no longer do what they think is the right thing for them to do, provide for their families. Maybe their wives have to go out and work. And maybe make more money than they do. Maybe the kids are running crazy because nobody's paying attention to them. Their lives are falling apart. They're angry. Who are they supposed to blame? You're not supposed to blame the Fortune 500, because they're invisible. They have been taught for fifty years now by intense propaganda, everything from the entertainment media to school books, that all there is around is the government. If there's anything going wrong, it's the government's fault. The government is somehow something that's independent of external powers. So if your life is falling apart, blame the government.

There are plenty of things wrong with the government. But what's harmful to people about the government is that it's a reflection of something else. And that other thing you don't see. Why don't you see that other thing? Because it's been made invisible. So when you read Clinton campaign propaganda you've got workers and their firms but not owners and investors. That's just the end result of fifty years of this stuff. Talking about your subtext, if people are angry and frightened, they will naturally turn to what they see. And what they've been taught to see is the government.

There's a reason why attention is focused on the government as the source of problems. It has a defect. It's potentially democratic. Private corporations are not potentially democratic. The propaganda system does not want to get people to think, The government is something we can take over and we can use as our instrument of public power. They don't want people to think that. And since you can't think that, you get what's called populism, but is not populism at all. It's not the kind of populism that says, Fine, let's take over the government and use it as an instrument to undermine and destroy private power, which has no right to exist. Nobody is saying that. All that you're hearing is that there's something bad about government, so let's blow up the federal building.

DB *I think the most interesting commentary on Oklahoma City was actually on CNN on April 25. They were interviewing Stanley Bedlington, who was identified as an ex-CIA counterterrorism specialist. He said, right after the bombing, that there was a potential for more violence. Why? Bedlington said, Because of "the deteriorating economic situation in rural America." I was stunned to hear that.*

It's not just rural America. These people that he's talking about happen to come from rural America. And it's true that out in rural America, where there are fewer controls, you may tend to get paramilitaries forming more than in the slums. But the problems are in New York City and in Boston and right throughout the whole mainstream of the country. The problems simply reflect very objective facts. Real wages have in fact been declining for fifteen years and profits are zooming. The country is splitting in a noticeably Third World pattern. There's a big superfluous population that nobody knows what to do with. So they toss them in jail. They want to make people afraid of them, so they're building up fear of crime and craziness about welfare. That's a real problem. Maybe in the rural counties is where they're going to form paramilitary groups, but this is going to be everywhere. He's right. It's a very big problem. It's a problem they face in every Third World country. That's why they have death squads and security forces. They have to face that problem of all those people they are just crushing under foot.

DB *Let's talk a little bit about conspiracy theories, because they're quite prevalent. In a curious way, your work and Holly Sklar's book on trilateralism are cited as evidence of conspiracy, somehow integrated with Freemasons and the Bilderbergers who all meet in the Bohemian Grove and the like. But it seems that if rhetoric is anti-regime, then there's just a suspension of critical inquiry. There's no insistence on evidence. Opinion is cited as proof. Then the chief arbiter or verifier is radio. "I heard it on the radio, therefore it's true."*

You're right. It's like that. I can see when I talk on right-wing radio that there's some degree of resonance of a kind to what I'm saying that I don't like. Bilderberg I've never mentioned. Bohemian Grove I don't care about. The Trilateral Commission I've mentioned a few times. I read their stuff all the time. It's so boring it's not worth looking at.

DB *But you talk about the de facto world government. That's what they talk about.*

I didn't talk about the de facto world government. I quoted it from The *Financial Times*. I said, The *Financial Times*, the world's leading business journal, is noticing that there is a de facto world government not of Freemasons, but of transnational corporations and institutions that they are spawning. So take a look at real centralized power, transnational corporations, who own most of the world. The Fortune 500 now has 63% of U.S. gross domestic product, and the transnationals have a huge proportion of world trade and investment in their hands. They are spawning a set of quasi-governmental institutions. The *Financial Times* lists them: the World Bank, the IMF, then it was the GATT Council, now it's the World Trade Organization. Sure, that's their picture, and it's a pretty accurate one. But that's not a conspiracy, any more than corporate boardrooms are a conspiracy.

DB *The left has certainly not been free from this. The Christic Institute theories about secret teams running around, and the numerous JFK assassination theories. I wonder what the left has to offer people like Timothy McVeigh and Mark Koernke. They are certainly not listening to Alternative Radio and not reading your books. How can we reach them?*

I think the left has to reach them by doing what the left failed to do the other night at the meeting we went to, when Decatur workers were coming here and asking for solidarity and support. That's where the left ought to be. I don't know Timothy McVeigh, but I think the left ought to be out there getting those guys to join unions and form grassroots organizations and take over their local governments. If the left can't do that, it doesn't deserve to exist.

DB *Just to explain, there was a Jobs with Justice meeting at MIT on May 9. Striking and locked-out workers from Decatur (there are three actions going on there) were there to bring this to the attention of people. There were only about 75 people in the hall. It was kind of distressing. In the same hall, in the last couple of months, when you gave talks on East Timor and Colombia and the drug war there were very large turnouts. What do you attribute the low attendance to?*

It could be technical things, like maybe there wasn't good publicity. I should say that this is the first talk that I've given in that big hall for probably twenty years which hasn't been virtually overflowing. This is also the first talk that happened to involve solidarity with working people. I doubt that that's a pure accident. I think that tells you something about where the left isn't and where it ought to be. There was one other meeting that was less well attended than I expected. It was on the Contract with America, which again involved welfare mothers and poor people.

DB *It's kind of hard to predict what's going to happen. There's that Yeats poem "The Second Coming": "Things fall apart; the centre cannot hold. Mere anarchy is loosed upon the world ... What rough beast ... Slouches toward Bethlehem to be born?" But in terms of Oklahoma City and now the call for a draconian increase in FBI powers of surveillance, infiltration, and the like, what do you think is coming up?*

Before Oklahoma City, Congress had already rescinded the Fourth Amendment, the elimination of the exclusionary law, allowing basically illegal search. That was prior to Oklahoma City. So Oklahoma City may somewhat extend FBI powers. I don't think it's going to have a big effect. I think the things that are happening lie elsewhere. The so-called conservatives want a powerful, violent state, and they want it to have a powerful security system. So during the 1980s, the U.S. prison population more than tripled. It's going up more. Under Clinton's crime bill it's going to go way up. The U.S. is virtually the only country—maybe Iraq, Iran, a few others—to let children be killed by the state, to have the death penalty for minors. The U.S. rarely signs international human rights conventions. We have a rotten record on that. But we just signed the International Convention on the Rights of the Child. We're the 177th country to sign it, which shows you how that goes. One of the provisions of that says that minors, meaning people under 19, cannot receive life imprisonment or the death penalty. We've got juveniles sitting on death row, so we're in straight violation of what we just signed. We're one of the very few countries that does that. This attack on the judicial system and the system of rights has nothing to do with Oklahoma City. It has to do with creating a much more punitive society which will deal somehow with the fact that an awful lot of people are useless for the one human value that still matters, namely, making profits. That's way more important than whatever further rights the FBI may get as a result of Oklahoma City, in my opinion. These things are bad, like Rush Limbaugh is bad. But there are much more central things that are happening.

DB *Earlier I said you had compared the current situation with Germany and Iran. What are your views on arguing by analogy? A lot of people all over the country were quick to bring up the Weimar Republic and even the Reichstag fire. Do you think that's a good way to understand things, to talk about analogies?*

Analogies can be helpful. You don't want to push them too hard. It's worth noticing that the kinds of circumstances that we see are not without historical precedent. It's not like they're coming from Mars. So there have been situations that are not identical. You can look crucially at the differences. But you can learn something from looking at history.

DB *What about the political uses of Islam and Muslims and Arabs in terms of what happened right after the Oklahoma City bombing?*

Take my "friend" A.M. Rosenthal. I'm surprised the *Times* is willing to let him loose. He gives you such an insight into how that newspaper was running for years when he was in charge of it. He writes a regular column. The day after Oklahoma City he had a column basically saying, This just shows that we're not dealing properly with Middle East terrorism. Let's bomb them all over the place. He said, We don't know yet who did it, but let's bomb the Middle East anyway. Not in those words, that was the message, to borrow your term, the "subtext." It wasn't very "sub," either. A couple of days later it turned out it was right-wing paramilitaries here. He wrote another column saying, This really shows that we're not dealing with terrorism from the Middle East properly, so let's be serious about it and deal with Middle East terrorism. They mean a very special kind of Middle East terrorism. They don't mean the kind, for example, when Israeli planes bomb villages in Lebanon and murder people. That's not terrorism they're talking about.

DB *Or the 1985 CIA bombing.*

They're not talking about the CIA bombing in Beirut, which is the one really close analog to Oklahoma City. The discipline of the media in "forgetting" the 1985 Beirut car bombing, the worst in history, specially targeting civilians, was pretty impressive, particularly with all the laments about how middle America was coming to look like Beirut and the hysterical threats to bomb anyone thought to be responsible—for Oklahoma City, not Beirut. The analogy was repeatedly brought to the attention of the press. That I know just from personal experience. But ears mysteriously closed. For those interested, I wrote about it in a book edited by Alex George called *Western State Terrorism*, a book unmentionable and unreviewable in the U.S., as one could predict from the title.

But they were not talking about the Beirut bombing that was virtually duplicated in Oklahoma City. Not even contemporary ones. Israel regularly bombs civilian targets in Lebanon. They don't pay attention to it. Occasionally you get a mention in the paper. Israel had Lebanon under blockade for a month. They wouldn't let fishermen out. Blockading a country is an act of aggression. In fact, Israel has a permanent blockade on Lebanon, from Tyre to the south. But nobody talks about that. It's all in violation of unanimous U.N. Security Council resolutions which now are almost twenty years old that the U.S. signed. That's not terrorism. In fact, they're not even talking about Turkey. First of all invading Iraq, but in its own southeast corner it's been carrying out murderous terrorism for years. It's getting worse and worse. They are not even talking about the actual terrorism that they're worried about.

Take Pan Am 103. Take a look at Iran. Iran is now supposed to be the center of international terrorism. Any time any act takes place, it's Iran. You don't even wait for evidence. With one extremely interesting exception: Pan Am 103 is not blamed on Iran. Why is that? How come that one example is not blamed on Iran? That's the one example which very likely Iran is involved in. So how come the one where Iran is most likely involved is not blamed on it? It's blamed on Libya, on very shaky grounds. I don't think it takes very long to figure that one out. It's very likely that the bombing of PanAm 103 was a retaliatory bombing for the shooting down of an Iranian Airbus by the American naval vessel *USS Vincennes* in the Persian Gulf, which was a straight act of murder. There have already been several articles in the *U.S. Naval Institute Proceedings*. The most recent one was by a retired Marine lieutenant colonel describing in detail what happened there. The commander of the *Vincennes* got the Legion of Merit for it. The ship just focused its high-tech weaponry on a commercial airliner, knowing it was a commercial airliner, right in commercial air space, and shot it down, killing 290 people. That was part of the U.S. tilt towards its friend Saddam Hussein during the Iraq-Iran war. That's not the kind of story that you want all over the front pages, so for that one act, Pan Am 103, Iran is not responsible, probably the one for which it *is* responsible.

So the concern over Middle East terrorism is highly selective in all sorts of ways, just like the concern over Islamic fundamentalism. The most fundamentalist state in the world is Saudi Arabia. I don't see a lot about that. Why? They do the job. They make sure the profits from oil come to the U.S., so they can be as fundamentalist as they like. This is the most shoddy and shallow propaganda. It's amazing they can get away with it.

DB *I've always wondered where you got access to the U.S. Naval Institute Proceedings. Is that sent to you? Do you subscribe to it?*

I look for it. I must have seen a reference somewhere and then went and looked. This story actually even finally made the mainstream press. *Newsweek* had a cover story on it two or three years ago. The first thing that I saw was something in the L.A. *Times*. The commander of the vessel next to the *Vincennes*, David Carlson, had an op-ed where he said, We were standing and watching in amazement. It happened to mention that he had an article in the *U.S. Naval Institute Proceedings*, so I looked it up. Then I started keeping my eyes on it and found this much more recent one on the Navy cover-up. This article goes through the cover-up. It even ends up quoting some high Army officer saying, The U.S. Navy shouldn't be allowed out on the high seas, they're too dangerous. That's not the kind of stuff you really want all over the place. It's kind of amazing that with all of the talk about Iran, right now we're embargoing Iran because they're involved in terrorism. It's a rogue state. Everybody's wild about Pan Am 103, and somehow you can't notice that that's the one thing that's not attributed to them and which they probably did.

Also quite interesting is the fact that the U.S. has charged several Libyans, but is making sure they don't go to trial. Libya has offered to have them tried in a neutral venue, like the Hague, but the U.S. and U.K. refuse—meaning they don't want them tried unless they can control the trial. The British committee of families of the victims has been militantly critical of this refusal. The U.S. committee just goes along with Washington propaganda, as does the U.S. press. A documentary about all this was played in the British Parliament and on BBC TV. Here, PBS refused to run it, and commercial TV isn't worth approaching. Try to find something about any of this in the media.

DB *You mentioned A.M. Rosenthal and his biases at the* Times. *But you don't have to go that far. Right here in Boston you have a talk show host, Howie Carr, who said that the Oklahoma City bombing was done by "a bunch of towelheads." There was a little story, though, in Oklahoma City involving an Iraqi woman, a refugee. Did you hear about that?*

I don't recall.

DB *Christopher Hitchens wrote about it in* The Nation. *It's one of* *the very few references I've seen. Saher Al-Saidi was seven months pregnant. Her house was attacked by a mob of rednecks screaming insults about Islam and Muslims. Windows were broken. She ran from room to room in fear and suffered a miscarriage.*

But that's not from Howie Carr. That's from years and years of perfectly mainstream publications presenting an image of Arab terrorists, Islamic fundamentalist crazies either attacking Israel or attacking us. The U.S. is in a state of national emergency now. President Clinton has declared a state of national emergency, because of the grave threat to our national security and national interest posed by Hezbollah in Lebanon and Hamas in the occupied territories. That's not Howie Carr.

DB *To continue with the political uses of Islam, Willy Claes, the NATO Secretary General in Brussels, in February said, "Islamic fundamentalism is just as dangerous as communism."*

Is he referring to Saudi Arabia? No. It's just like liberation theology. Anything that's out of control is dangerous. If there's some brand of Islamic fundamentalism that's out of control, that's dangerous. If there's some brand of the Catholic church that's out of control, that's dangerous. If it's a democratic politician in Guatemala who's out of control, that's dangerous. If you're out of control you're dangerous. Islamic fundamentalism is one of the ways in which a very repressed part of the world is beginning to organize itself independently. So naturally that's unacceptable. And it's not Islamic fundamentalism. You can tell that right off. The leading Islamic fundamentalist state is Saudi Arabia. Let's go away from states. Take non-state actors. Who are the most extreme Islamic fundamentalists in the world? The ones who the U.S. supported in Afghanistan for ten years. They would beat anybody. Gulbuddin Hekmatyar. You can't get beyond that. He makes Saudi Arabia look mild. He got $6 billion of aid from the U.S. and Saudi Arabia. Right now he has been tearing the country apart. This isn't Pol Pot. You don't get any points for talking about the atrocities after the Americans pulled out. Here the Russians pulled out, and as soon as the Russians pulled out they started destroying the place. But it's our guys destroying it. So therefore you have to look pretty hard to find it. Kabul has been wrecked. Thousands, maybe tens of thousands of people have been killed. Maybe hundreds of thousands of refugees.

Mostly guys like Gulbuddin Hekmatyar, our man, bombarding the place. Afghanistan has become one of the major centers of drug production. Our guys, they are fanatic Islamic fundamentalists, but we certainly weren't worrying about them when we were pouring money into their pockets.

DB *And that CIA operation in Afghanistan has spilled over into Pakistan, where there's severe drug addiction. You've written about this. Benazir Bhutto is now asking the U.S. to help with Pakistan's terrorist problem.*

One thing I would mention is that when it's a CIA operation, that means it's a White House operation. It's not CIA. They don't do things on their own.

DB *That's a point you made about the recent disclosures about Guatemala.*

Let's be serious about it. Maybe you'll find a rogue operation now and then, but as far as I'm aware, overwhelmingly the CIA does what it's told by the White House. So its role is to provide plausible denial for the White House, and people shouldn't fall for that game. If it's a CIA operation it's because they were ordered to do it. They're only part of the operation.

DB *I've got a flight in less than an hour. My mind is going to the airport, so I'm not all here, but let's just continue this for a few minutes longer. I want to ask you about the selective use of memory. I remember my mother telling me about her village in Turkish Armenia. It was paradise. I never heard a negative thing said about anything. Everyone was living in a sort of Edenesque country there. But thinking about you in the 1940s in Philadelphia with your family, what kind of information were you getting about what the Nazis were up to in Europe? Did you have a sense of what was unfolding there?*

You mean in the 1930s?

DB *Not just in the 1930s, but the genocide.*

Everybody knew more or less what was going on. By 1943 at the latest it was pretty well known what was happening, and there was at least the beginning of a public outcry. Even before the war, the sense of growing terror was palpable in my parents' circles. But take the 1930s, speaking of memories. The other night in the meeting on Decatur they showed a video on police violence. I remember that very well from 1934-1935, with much worse scenes of police attacking. I remember I was with my mother on a trolley car. I must have been five years old. There was a textile strike. Women workers were picketing. We just passed by and saw a very violent police attack on women strikers, picketers outside, much worse than what we saw the other night in the video on Decatur, which was bad enough. So idyllic memories of childhood, I think one has to ask some questions about. In the 1930s it was pretty clear that the Nazis were a very ominous and dangerous force that was like a dark cloud over everything throughout my whole childhood. By the early 1940s, around the middle of the war, it was pretty obvious, maybe you didn't know the details about Auschwitz, but the general picture was pretty clear.

DB *You were reading voraciously in those days. I think there's a comment in the film* Manufacturing Consent *where you used to check out ten, twelve, fourteen books at a time from the library.*

Remember, in those days there were good library systems. That was one of the reasons you could survive the Depression. But I spent a lot of time at the downtown Philadelphia public library. It was the big public library that had everything. You couldn't check books out from there because they didn't allow it. But I was reading plenty of stuff, a lot of odd dissident journals, some of them crackpot, some of them interesting. All sorts of material.

DB *Again, bringing it to today, you encourage people to be skeptical. You often end a talk, Don't believe anything I say. Go and find out for yourself. When does that skepticism, which I suggest is happening with some of these paramilitaries, switch into paranoia?*

Skepticism can lead to paranoia, but it certainly doesn't have to. Any good scientist is skeptical all the time. Every time a professional journal comes in, the students read it with skepticism, if they're any good, at least, because they know you've got to question and evaluate. But when you read a technical journal with skepticism, that doesn't mean you assume it's being prepared by the Bilderberg conference to undermine your mind. That's quite a gap. The difference is that skepticism against a background of understanding and rationality is a very healthy attitude. Skepticism against a vacuum is extremely dangerous. The educational system and the doctrinal system have created vacuums. People's minds are empty and confused because everything's been driven out of them. In that case skepticism can quickly turn into paranoia.

DB *But there is a drumbeat of propaganda constantly going on. You sort of dismissed Limbaugh and what he represents, but he reaches twenty million listeners. We don't have that kind of audience.*

We don't, but commercial television and Hollywood have a much bigger audience. I'm not dismissing Limbaugh. I'm saying that that's a peripheral phenomenon. Let's take the kind of things, when I was a young adult, I was seeing in the movies, like *On the Waterfront*, a big, famous movie. That was typical of a genre. Tens of millions of dollars were put into making films like that, all of them with the same message. The message is, Unions are the enemy of the working man. The theme of that movie is Marlon Brando, upstanding, courageous young guy, throws union boss into the ocean and stands up for his rights. That was the key picture of very self-conscious propaganda running through the entertainment industry, the schools, the newspapers, everything else, saying, We are on one side, "we" being the working folks, like the guy who happens to sit in the executive office and the guy on the assembly line, we're all on one side. Then there are the really bad guys trying to destroy our lives, namely, the outsiders, the unions. We've got to defend ourselves from them. That has worked. That has led to the present situation.

Take a look at popular attitudes. I think about 80% of the population think that working people don't have enough influence. A substantial number think that unions have too much influence. After NAFTA, the opinions were opposed to NAFTA on the same grounds that the labor unions opposed it, but they were opposed to the labor unions for having involved themselves in that dispute, namely, in advocating the positions that most of the population supported. That wasn't Rush Limbaugh. That's the result of decades—it goes back to the nineteenth century, but I mean in the modern period—of very intensive propaganda designed to make people lose the sense of solidarity and sympathy and mutual support and help for one another and democratization that unions stand for. When you wipe that degree of understanding and sympathy and support out of people's heads, then you go right to paranoia. It's that kind of thing that a demagogue like Limbaugh can exploit, but I think we should recognize where the problem lies. Not there. Much deeper. He wouldn't get anywhere if he didn't have this basis prepared for it.

DB *I'm not going to say "subtext," but another theme, I wonder if you're aware of this. The director of* On the Waterfront *was Elia Kazan. He sang to the House Un-American Activities Committee. Marlon Brando plays a character who is encouraged to and is justified in cooperating with the authorities.*

Elia Kazan was one of the people who was subjected to the McCarthyite routine, and yes, he sang to the House Un-American Activities Committee. I don't have any comment on that. You don't blame people for not being heroes, for just being ordinary people. So I think he could have been more courageous than that, like, say, Lillian Hellman, but that's easy for me to say. So, yes, he did. And it's true that's what happened. But that was just the most successful of a genre. It was kind of interesting. I think that movie came out the same year as *Salt of the Earth*, which is a very serious, low-budget but excellently done film. It's a thousand times as good as *On the Waterfront* from any esthetic or other criteria, except it happened to be pro-union. It showed in a few small theaters around. That's not the message that the multi-billion dollar entertainment industry was being organized to put across at that time. That's a dramatic contrast, and it's by no means the only one. That's just typical of decades of propaganda.

DB *What do you have coming up in terms of trips and books? I know you have a new linguistics book that MIT is putting out. Any political books coming out?*

I hope so. I promised a couple, anyway. I was in Australia for a week and I promised them that I would write up the talks and they'll publish it and maybe somebody will here. It's on a lot of different things. Then I also promised South End that I would try to write up and expand this series of articles on "Rollback" that's been running in

Z magazine.

DB *How about your book on the Middle east,* Fateful Triangle*? You've been talking about revising that as well.*

There have been many requests to update and revise it. Actually, the third chapter of the book of mine that just came out (*World Orders Old and New*), about a third of that book is kind of an updating. But I might want to do that. There's a lot to say about the region.

The Federal Reserve Board

May 31, 1995

DB *Wednesday is usually, I forget, is it your golf or tennis day?*

Both. [laughs]

DB *I hate to remind you of things, Noam, but 1995 marks your fortieth year at MIT.*

That's right, just finishing it.

DB *How did you get that job?*

When I got out of four years at Harvard and the Society of Fellows, I had basically no formal profession, no credentials in any formal academic field, and had no particular commitment to the academic world. I wasn't at all sure I was going to even try to continue. But I had some friends at MIT. Morris Halle, you know him?

DB *Of course, he has an office right across the hall from yours.*

We had been friends already for years as graduate students. He was here, doing part-time research and part-time teaching. There was a project at the Research Lab of Electronics on machine translation which had an interest in linguists. So he and Roman Jakobson helped a bit. I met with the director of the laboratory. We talked a little bit about it. I said I would be happy to come but I wouldn't work on that project, which I didn't think had any interest for me, but I would be glad to come to do the kind of work that I was interested in and to do some teaching and so on. They thought that was fine. So I came and did the work I was interested in at the Research Lab of Electronics, the same place where I am now, this old Second World War wooden building. I started doing a little teaching on the side.

Within about five years Morris and I had managed to arrange

some things. People began being interested from outside. Visitors came. We pretty soon had a doctoral candidate who we had to put through the electrical engineering department because we didn't have any department at the time. In 1960, I guess, we managed to start the official department.

DB *You've commented to me that when you joined MIT at around that time there was a group of you that were politically active and committed.*

Not at that time. At that time it was basically unknown. In fact, I wouldn't swear to this, but I think that I was the first person at the laboratory who refused to be cleared. It was a military-financed laboratory, and people routinely went through security clearance procedures. I just refused. I know everyone thought it was kind of weird, because the only effect of it was that I missed out on free trips on military air transport and things like that. It was considered strange enough that I suspect that I must have been the first person ever to do that. I didn't know any politically active people here at all.

DB *So that came later, people like Wayne O'Neil and others.*

That's ten years later.

DB *Did you feel that you had any allies internally?*

Internally? Political allies? No, not really. I didn't expect to. My political life was somewhere else. I should say that within a few years I did meet people on the faculty who themselves had pretty similar interests and backgrounds to mine, some older people, for example Salvador Luria, a Nobel-Prize-winning biologist. I've forgotten whether he was here when I came. He was certainly here within a few years. He was older. But we shared plenty of interests. We must have met in the early 1960s. And there were other people. My friend Louis Kampf, and quite a few others. By the early 1960s people were kind of getting together.

DB *That research you were doing in the 1950s and 1960s, was any of it federally funded?*

Oh, yeah. Not only was it federally funded, it was militarily funded. In fact, whether anything is military-funded or not is pretty much a bookkeeping exercise. MIT runs primarily on soft money, not on endowments, not on tuition. How the soft money is distributed is a very mysterious matter which they don't even understand in the bookkeeping department, as I know, having once been on a committee that tried to look into it years later. In a certain sense, everything is military-funded, even the music department. The sense in which that's true is that if they didn't have military funding for, say, the electrical engineering department and had to go to other funds for that, that would cut off the departments like the music department. So it is primarily a bookkeeping matter. But if you look at books of mine that were written in the early 1960s, you'll notice a formal statement on the front page saying, This was funded with the support of, and then it lists the three services. The reason is that the laboratory itself is funded by the three services, or was, maybe still is, for all I know.

DB *How has the institution changed over the time that you have been there?*

The big change was to a certain extent a result of the changes in science and math education in the country that took place around 1960. To some extent it was sparked by Sputnik, or at least that was used as the pretext for it. That created a great concern in Congress and around the country that somehow we were falling behind the Russians. That initiated and maybe was exploited for (you can argue about this) a lot of involvement in science education and math education in the schools. Within a short period of time students were coming to MIT who were much better trained. MIT started to shift at that time, more or less as a reflection of the students who were coming in, from an engineering school, which it had been in the 1950s—when I got here it was primarily an engineering school—to a science-math school, which it was by the mid-1960s. So many more students were majoring in the core sciences and mathematics. The classical engineering disciplines started to decline, people who were figuring out how to build bridges and things like that. Students were much less interested in that. The engineering departments that remained generally duplicated science curricula. So like in the electrical engineering department you wouldn't be studying how to put circuits together, but you would be studying physics and mathematics not unlike what you would be studying in the physics and math departments, except with applications to electrical engineering problems. The same is true of aeronautical engineering and mechanical engineering and so on. It became a science-based university instead of an engineering-based one.

One consequence of this was a considerable growth in the humanities. The engineers of the 1950s were pretty vocationally oriented. For them the humanities were kind of a frill. It was something you took so that you could know how to talk to people politely. But by the 1960s, the science and math students, for one thing, had more time. They weren't totally occupied with applications, and they just had other interests. That led to student pressure to expand the humanities programs. I was personally interested in that myself, especially with philosophy, so I was particularly involved in trying to develop the philosophy program from being kind of like a prep school, read-some-interesting-books type of program, to a real philosophy program, both undergraduate and graduate.

The same happened in history. At about that time, other departments were spinning off. The biology and psychology and brain sciences departments all spun off at that time, actually from the very same electronics laboratory. The electronics laboratory where I was was a place where there was a very strange and complicated mixture of people interested in all sorts of offbeat topics, which later became departments, some of them huge, at the Institute. Biology and psychology and linguistics and philosophy and the computer sciences all came out of that milieu. But by the mid-1960s it was a very different sort of place, like a university based on science rather than a high-quality engineering school. You could see the shift in the nature of the students, the curricula, etc.

It was still very apolitical, in a sense. I should say that the faculty peace activities in this area, signing ads, organizing protests, were mostly based at MIT, not at Harvard, from the early 1960s. So even though overall the Institute has a more conservative cast than, say, Harvard, it's here that the political activists mostly work. A few people drifted in on the periphery from Harvard, Howard Zinn from Boston University, but it was mainly MIT, even though it's a very small group of faculty. Among the students, there was a small group, people like Mike Albert and Steve Shalom and others, who were students around the mid-1960s. They were very active starting around 1965, 1966.

Also Louis Kampf and I were teaching at the time very large undergraduate courses with hundreds of students on contemporary affairs and social and political issues, the role of intellectuals, alternative vocations, things like that. They were bringing in lots of students as the ferment of the 1960s finally hit MIT. But it really wasn't until late 1968 or early 1969 that the Institute became really seriously politicized and became seriously involved in things like the antiwar movement and so on.

DB *You often give talks at MIT. Just in the last few months you've given talks on Colombia and the drug war, East Timor, and most recently in solidarity with the workers in Decatur, Illinois.*

This role of MIT as the central place for community and university-based activism has continued. So if an organization wants to have a meeting, they're much more likely to have it here than at Harvard or Boston University. Much more likely. That's why we always have these meetings where you show up at the same room, 26-100.

DB *The new CIA director is John Deutch. He's a former MIT provost. Did you know him?*

Not terribly well, but we knew each other.

DB *The reason I'm asking is that I figure when you retire from MIT you'll have a new career at Langley (CIA headquarters).*

I don't think so [chuckles]. We were actually friends and got along fine, although we disagreed on about as many things as two human beings can disagree about. I liked him. We got along very well together. He's very honest, very direct. You know where you stand with him. We talked to each other. When we had disagreements, they were open, sharp, clear, honestly dealt with. I found it fine. I had no problem with him. I was one of the very few people on the faculty, I'm told, who was supporting his candidacy for the President of MIT.

DB *Which he didn't get, right?*

There was faculty opposition.

DB *One of the questions you are often asked after your talks is the one about, How can you work at MIT? You've never had any interference with your work, have you?*

Quite the contrary. MIT has been very supportive. In the 1960s, particularly, I'm sure I was giving them plenty of trouble. I don't know the figures now, but in 1969, when the only serious faculty/student inquiry into this was undertaken, into funding, there was a commission set up at the time of local ferment about military labs, and I was on it, and at that time MIT funding was almost entirely the Pentagon. About half the Institute's budget was coming from two major military laboratories that they administered, and of the rest, the academic side, it could have been something like 90% or so from the Pentagon. Something like that. Very high. So it was a Pentagon-based university. And I was at a military-funded lab.

But I never had the slightest interference with anything I did. MIT had quite a good record on protecting academic freedom. I'm sure that they were under pressure, maybe not from the government, but certainly from alumni, I would imagine. I was very visible at the time in organizing protests and resistance. You know the record. It was very visible and pretty outspoken and far out. But we had no problems from them, nor did anyone, as far as I know, draft resisters, etc.

DB *That always surprises people when you tell them that.*

It shouldn't. It just shows that they don't understand how things work. A science-based university like this is much freer in those respects.

DB *Let's talk about some economic issues. I want to start with the Federal Reserve. What is its role?*

The Federal Reserve basically controls things like interest rates. It's had various commitments or directives over the years. Originally its official goals, at least, were to keep inflation down and employment up. So one of its goals was to help achieve the goal of effectively full employment. That never means a hundred percent, but something approaching it. That goal has receded into the distance. Now its primary commitment is to preventing inflation. That's a reflection of things that have happened in international financial markets. So the amount of unregulated financial capital in the world has exploded astronomically in the last twenty-five years. It moves around very fast, thanks to telecommunications and so on. So there may be, let's say, a trillion dollars a day moving around financial markets. It's mostly speculating against currencies. It moves to places where it looks as though currencies are going to be stable with high unemployment and low economic growth, so that there are unlikely to be inflationary pressures. The Federal Reserve has been basically anti-inflation. If you are investing, say, in bonds, your biggest enemy is potential inflation, which means potential growth. Therefore you want to move away from places which are going to be stimulating the economy. The Federal Reserve interest rates will tend to go up to prevent stimulation of the economy and the possibility of inflation—the two tend to go together. So they've had a dampening effect on economic growth, also on jobs. They want unemployment to go up, basically. So unemployment goes up, the labor costs go down. There's less pressure for wage increases. So the commitment to full employment, which was originally at least part of their formal commitment, has disappeared.

DB *There's an interesting comment that Paul Volcker made in 1979. He was the head of the Fed then. He said the living standard of the average American has to decline. That's one policy that has certainly produced results.*

But it's not just the Fed. This is part of general processes going on in the domestic and international economy and also very specific social policies. You don't have to react to them this way. For example, there are ways to slow down the movement of financial capital and to protect currencies and to maintain stimulative policies by government. There are ways to do that, and those ways have been known for a long time. They're not undertaken because of a commitment to certain social policies. Those social policies are basically to roll back the welfare state. There's a pretty good article on this, if you're interested, in the current issue of *Challenge* magazine, a good journal of economics, written by a very fine international economist, David Felix. It's on what's called the Tobin tax. This is a proposal made by James Tobin back in 1978, a Nobel Prize-winning economist at Yale. This was a well-known talk he gave. He was then President of the American Economic Association. This was his presidential address. This was the early stages of the process, but he pointed out that the flow of financial capital and the increase of it is going to have the effect of driving down growth rates and wages and it will also have a further effect of increasing inequality, concentrating wealth in narrower sectors of the population. He suggested at the time a tax, which would have to be international, which would penalize movement of financial funds just for speculation against currency. That's called the Tobin tax. It's been kicking around the UN for some years, but it's never been implemented. David Felix's point in this article is that, nobody knows for sure, but it could very well work, it could very well shift capital from economically useless speculative purposes, in fact, economically destructive speculative purposes, to more productive investment. It could very well have that effect. But even the sectors of private capital that would benefit from it have not supported it. He argues that the reason is that they have an overriding class interest, which overcomes their narrow profit interest. The overriding class interest is to use the fiscal crisis of states to undermine the social contract that's been built up—to roll back the gains in welfare, union rights, labor rights, and so on. That interest is sufficient that they are willing to see this instrument used to cut back growth in investment, even the sectors that would benefit from it. It is a pretty plausible argument, I think. And the Federal Reserve is just a piece of it.

DB *The Fed is kind of the de facto central bank of the U.S. But it's private, right?*

No, it's not private. It's independent of specific government orders. The President can't order it to do something. But its members and director are appointed through the government.

DB *So they're presidential appointments?*

Yes. But then they're essentially independent.

DB *It seems that the Fed and other central banks can't seem to stabilize and control currency rates as they once could.*

That's gone because the system was dismantled. There was a system up until the early 1970s.

DB *Bretton Woods.*

Yes.

DB *But there was this recent precipitous drop of the dollar against the yen and the mark, for example. The banks tried to stabilize the dollar ...*

It's not clear that they tried. Maybe the European banks did. It's not at all clear that the American government did, or its banks. It's just not at all obvious that that was their goal. They may be happy to see the dollar drop.

DB *But it is your contention that traders and speculators command more capital today than the central banks?*

I don't think it's my contention. It's everybody's contention.

DB *David Peterson alerted me to a passage in John Maynard Keynes's classic work from the mid-1930s,* The General Theory of Employment, Interest, and Money. *Keynes says: "As the organization of investment markets improves, the risk of the predominance of speculation does, however, increase. Speculators may do no harm as bubbles on a steady stream of enterprise, but the position is serious when enterprise becomes the bubble on a whirlpool of speculation."*

That's happened. That's why the Bretton Woods system, which Keynes was instrumental in helping to craft, did have mechanisms for regulation of currencies. The basic idea of the system was that the dollar was the international currency in those days because of the overwhelming industrial and economic power of the U.S., which was indeed overwhelming. So the dollar was the international currency. It was fixed relative to gold. Then other currencies were regulated relative to the dollar. There were various devices to allow a certain degree of flexibility, depending on economic growth, recession, and so on. That was the fundamental system. That was dismantled unilaterally by the U.S. in the early 1970s, when the U.S. determined that it no longer wanted to function as basically the international banker. This had to do with a lot of things: the growth of the more or less trilateral economic system (with the growth of the Japanese-based system and the growth of the German-based European system), and also the cost of the Vietnam War and its economic benefits to rivals of the U.S. These led to these decisions by the Nixon administration.

At the time that these decisions were made, financial speculation was a bubble. So estimates are that about ten percent of the capital in international exchanges at the time was for speculation and about ninety percent was related to the real economy, for investment and trade. By the 1990 those figures were reversed. It was about ninety percent speculation and ten percent investment and trade. David Felix did a recent study done for UNCTAD, the United Nations Conference on Trade and Development, in which he cites estimates that by 1994 it was about ninety-five percent speculative and about five percent real economy-related. So that's pretty much what Keynes was worried about.

DB *To continue with Keynes, he said, "When the capital development of a country becomes a byproduct of the activities of a casino, the job is likely to be ill-done."*

By the 1980s, the international economy was being called a "casino economy." There is a book with that title by a well-known British international economist, Susan Strange, *The Casino Economy*. And others were using the same phrase. It becomes in thrall to speculation. It's this that James Tobin was warning about in 1978, when the whole process was still in its early stages.

DB *Do you think the current economic system can continue in this cycle of ups and downs, or is it prone to collapse? Have they built in enough safeguards to protect themselves from another 1929?*

Nobody has the slightest idea. In the early 1980s, when the debt crisis hit, the banks were worried that they wouldn't be able to contain it. They were bailed out by the public. The huge Third World debt, which had been developed very fast, became a major problem when U.S. interest rates shot up, since a lot of the debt is keyed to the dollar. As interest rates shot up, for one thing, a ton of money began flowing out of places like Latin America. Not East Asia, because East Asia has capital controls. So rich Koreans couldn't send their capital to the U.S. There are controls on that. But the wealth of Latin America, which is much more open to international markets for various historical reasons, simply flowed to U.S. banks. This led to a complete collapse in Latin America. In fact, the debt owed by Latin America is not all that different from the amount of capital flight from Latin America. Also, the interest rates on the debt went way up because they're tied to U.S. interest rates.

Then came this huge debt crisis. It looked like major countries, Brazil, Mexico, and others, were going to default. The big banks were very worried. That was finessed mainly by a taxpayer bailout. It was picked up by the World Bank. One way or another, most of the debt was transferred over to the public domain and the banks were bailed out.

In 1987 there was another apparent crisis. We just saw one in December 1994. Nobody knew what the domino effect might be of the Mexican collapse, whether it was going to start toppling other Third World financial markets, which are also based very heavily on speculation, just as the Mexican one was. The Clinton bailout was not so much to pay off the people who invested through speculation in Mexico. They had already pulled out their money or lost it. It was to prop up export capital to countries like Argentina and so on and to guarantee people against losses there. So it is a taxpayer bailout going to promote relatively risk-free investment through public funds, but not so much for the Mexican investors. This one seems to have been contained, too. But what will happen next time I don't think anybody knows. Predictions on this are almost meaningless. Just take a look at what the international economists and the World Bank were predicting about Mexico, and that will tell you how reliable their forecasts are. Up until the collapse, they were just euphoric about the prospects for Mexico, this great economic miracle. After the collapse they started explaining how they knew it all along. But try to find it before.

DB *To get back to the whole issue of employment, there was a notion in the U.S. that full employment was a desirable policy goal. That has changed dramatically.*

There no longer is even a theoretical commitment to full employment, as there had been from the late 1940s. There was a commitment, at least a theoretical commitment, which was sometimes partially implemented from the late 1940s on, but that's gone. Now the commitment is to something different. It's to what's called the "natural rate of unemployment." There's supposed to be some natural rate. As unemployment goes down below some natural rate of unemployment, then inflation is supposed to go up, and you want to make sure that unemployment stays at the natural place. People differ on what that is, but it's pretty high, over six percent.

DB *That's a pretty bogus figure.*

It's not bogus. It has a certain meaning. It means that you want wages to stay low enough so that they don't carry the risk of potential inflation.

DB *I say bogus in that a lot of people are simply not counted.*

But that's always been true. What they call unemployment is a figure well below the number of unemployed. That's always true. There are people who are off the labor market or who have given up, who are out of the visible economy. So these are just the numbers. That was also true when they were aiming at three percent.

DB *Even if you work one hour a week, for example, you're considered employed.*

I wouldn't say "bogus," because everybody knows the way it's done. The numbers measure something. They certainly don't measure the number of people who have a regular job that they want.

DB *There seem to be some obvious advantages to corporate power to have a permanent army of the unemployed.*

Although we should bear in mind that by now they have an international army of the unemployed. During the latest recession, the Clinton recovery, this growth period of the last couple of years, there has not been a corresponding growth in wages, even though employment has gone up, which is what you'd expect in a normal labor market. As the employment goes up and the reserve army of unemployed goes down, you'd expect the pressure on wages to go up. But that hasn't happened. Nobody knows for certain, but it's probable that a large part of the reason for that is that there always is the threat of simply transferring production elsewhere. You don't even have to implement the threat. The fact that it's there is enough.

There's nothing abstract about this. Take, say, the current strikes in Decatur, a crucial moment in labor history. Three major corporations, only one of which is based in the U.S. (one is based in Britain and one in Japan) are involved in trying to basically destroy some of the last remnants of the industrial labor unions in the U.S. in this old working-class town. One of them is a strict lockout. The other two are technically strikes—"were," I should say, because the United Auto Workers have already collapsed. So there are only two still going. The others are strikes, but they're strikes that the corporations wanted, because they wanted to be able to destroy the unions.

They've explained how they could do it. Caterpillar, the U.S.-based one, first of all has profits coming out of its ears. It's making huge profits, like other major corporations, so it's got plenty of capital. There's no problem that way. But furthermore, they've been using their profits over the past years to build up excess capacity in other countries. For example, they have plants in Brazil where they can get much cheaper labor and they can keep filling their international orders. Notice that that's not done for reasons of economic efficiency. Quite the contrary. It's done for power reasons. You don't build up excess capacity for economic efficiency, but you do build it up for power reasons, as a threat against the domestic work force. And this is true in case after case.

Take another current example. It indicates that this is not abstract. It's very real. It is the trade war that's going on with Japan. Have a close look at it. The U.S. is trying to get Japan to open its markets to auto parts manufactured by U.S. manufacturers. That's the big issue. But when the *Wall Street Journal* interviewed the CEOs of the corporations that make the parts, they said of course they'd be delighted to have the Japanese markets open. But they said that they would not supply them from U.S. plants. They would mostly supply them from plants in Asia. Because they've built up a network of producers elsewhere where they again get much cheaper workers and, of course, are much closer to the Japanese market. So if Japan capitulates in this conflict, it's not (according to the *Wall Street Journal* analysis, at least) very likely that there will be many more American jobs, though there will be plenty more American profits.

DB *Why is Clinton pushing Japan now?*

He would like to see the U.S. auto makers and their investors make more profits.

DB *What might happen if the World Trade Organization hears this case and it goes against the U.S.?*

GATT, which was the predecessor of the World Trade Organization, has ruled against the U.S. on a number of occasions. They just don't pay any attention. And nobody is going to put any pressure on the U.S. It's just too big. There are mechanisms in the international trade organizations. GATT and the World Trade Organization have methods to penalize countries that don't play by the rules. But just remember what the methods are. For example, if, say, Nicaragua objects to U.S. violations of the GATT rules, as it did, and if GATT concludes that Nicaragua is right, as it did, Nicaragua is then completely free to penalize the U.S. by raising its tariffs on U.S. imports, let's say. That's not even a joke. On the other hand, if the U.S. wants to do something to Nicaragua, they can kill it, by the same rules. But who's going to try to close their markets to U.S. exports?

DB *A couple of months ago we talked about the World Court case involving Portugal and Australia on East Timor oil. Is there any update on that?*

There won't be for several months. The litigation was completed around early February. Then the court takes a number of months to reach a decision. People are guessing probably in the fall. It won't be very easy to keep informed. As far as I'm aware—I haven't checked it in the data base—but I haven't seen any reference to the World Court case in the U.S.

DB *How did you hear about it?*

I know about it from other sources. For one thing, it's all over the Australian, Portuguese, and European press.

DB *At a talk you gave at MIT on May 9th for the striking and locked-out workers in Decatur, you made a couple of interesting comments that I'd like you to expand on. You said the current political climate in the U.S. "is kind of an organizer's dream. ... It's a situation in which the* *opportunities for organizing and rebuilding a democratic culture are very, very high." What's the basis of your optimism?*

Actually, to give credit where it's due, I was stealing a line from my friend Mike Albert, who made that comment. I think the comment is accurate. There is a general mood of fear and concern and disillusionment and cynicism and recognition that things aren't going right which is based in reality. For maybe eighty percent of the population living standards have either been stagnant or have actually declined over the last fifteen years or so. They don't see any hope of anything better. Their anger is mostly focused on government, not on the Fortune 500. But that's the result of very effective propaganda over many years, which kind of puts in the shadow the source of decision making. But the concerns are there. If they can be mobilized, there could be a very constructive response. Again, let's make it concrete. Take these people who call themselves "militias." They're not militias, of course. Militias are things set up by states. But these paramilitary organizations that are called militias—people like the Timothy McVeighs, assuming that the government's story is accurate—if you look at those people, who are they? They're mostly white, working-class men with something like high school educations. They're the pretty much the kind of people who were building the CIO sixty years ago. Why aren't they doing something similar now? It's an organizer's dream, but they're not being organized.

DB *Right.*

In fact, you remember in the meeting, when the worker from Staley was talking?

DB *Very well.*

I thought he gave a very eloquent talk. I don't know if you have it on tape, but if you do you ought to play it. He's describing his picture of what he wanted his life to be and thought it ought to be. I'll bet you that if you were to pick a person at random from those paramilitary groups, you'd get the same picture or something similar to it. If people like the guy who was talking are driven—if that life is taken away from them, and the possibilities of their having a meaningful existence with serious work and family life and the rest of what he was saying—there's nothing unreasonable that he was asking for, not at all.

In fact, it was praiseworthy. But if those possibilities are taken away, they're going to go in one of two directions. Either they too will be doing something like joining paramilitary groups, or some other destructive activity (there are plenty of possibilities) or they will be the people who will rebuild the civil society that's being dismantled and restore some semblance of a democratic system. The differences between him and the people in the paramilitary groups I think are differences of commitment and understanding, not so much a social background or even goals, necessarily.

DB *I noticed particularly after you came back from Australia in late January your spirits were really up and you had a lot of energy. It seems to have sustained itself through this whole spring period. Am I seeing you correctly?*

I don't know. It was a kind of a shot in the arm in many ways. It was sort of exhilarating. But I doubt that it would have been very different. There's a kind of natural cycle of activism and things to do and energy and a decline as things quiet down.

DB *Your academic year is almost over.*

But it's not just the academic year. The point is that the rhythm of activism in the U.S., meaning organized activities, meetings, talks, and so on, that's pretty correlated with the academic year. So things do die down around June.

DB *Are you looking forward to the summer at Wellfleet, on the Cape?*

Yes. Plenty of work to do. It'll be good to be away for a bit, and I've got a ton of things to do.

DB *And you get a little sailing and swimming in on the side?*

I hope so. We'll see.

DB *See you at the Z Media Institute in Woods Hole in a few weeks. Take care.*

Take from the Needy and Give to the Greedy

October 31 and November 3, 1995

DB *You've been following the World Court case, the Timor Gap Treaty involving Portugal and Australia. What's happened with that?*

On June 30th the World Court announced its decision, actually non-decision. It decided to evade the issue. There were procedural issues, like, Can they go ahead at all with Indonesia not there, and then if they had agreed to that there would have been the substantive issues, but they stopped on the procedural issues. On a vote of 12-3, they said that they could not proceed without Indonesia present, so the issue's dead. On the other hand, if you read the whole ruling, it's not completely empty. For example, they did say that there can be no doubt under international law that East Timor has the inalienable right of self-determination; but they said they can't proceed any further on the technical matter of the treaty without one of the parties present, and Indonesia refuses to take part, just like the U.S. on Nicaragua. In Nicaragua they did go ahead, but on this one they didn't.

DB *You've commented on the relative power of Australia vis-à-vis Portugal in arguing this case.*

I haven't seen the whole record, but what I saw of Portugal's case didn't look to me very impressive. And Australia had (again, what I saw of it) they did it cleverly in the legal sense. After all, we have to remember that even at the World Court or the Supreme Court the law is to a considerable extent a sort of duel where truth and significance are around the fringes somewhere. A lot of it is show and technique. One thing that Australia brought up that embarrassed Portugal a lot, although it's irrelevant, had to do with their dealings with Morocco and Western Sahara, which the Australians brought up to show, You're just being hypocritical. Two seconds' worth of thought shows that whether they're being hypocritical or not has zero to do with this case. But in the court deliberations and the colloquy they apparently have a lot to do with it. That's standard courtroom procedure. And the Australians seemed pretty good at that. It's a First World country, and they know how to play these games.

DB *I'm not familiar with the Portuguese position. Are they in favor of the Moroccan annexation of Western Sahara?*

I don't know the exact details, but they apparently made some kind of deal with Morocco about maybe Western Saharan minerals or something. The Australians brought this up and said, This is a parallel, so how can you even bring up the case of East Timor? At most what it shows is that Portugal is hypocritical, which is not the issue. But as courts work, it was an issue.

DB *You've just returned from a series of talks in Washington and Oregon. There were the by now customary huge turnouts and standing ovations and the like. But I sense you feel some disquiet. What's that about?*

To tell you the honest truth, when I see a huge mob, which is pretty common these days, I have a mixture of feelings. Partly I'm sort of depressed about it, for a lot of reasons. For one thing, there's just too much personalization. It doesn't make any sense. It's worrisome. The other thing is that the ratio of passive participation to active engagement is way too high. These were well-arranged talks. For example, they did what a lot of people don't do and ought to do. Every place I went there were a dozen tables outside with every conceivable organization having leaflets and handouts and sign-up sheets and telling what they're up to. So if people want to do anything there are easy answers to what you can do in your own community. The question that comes up over and over again, and I don't really have an answer still, (really, I don't know any other people who have answers to them), is, It's terrible, awful, getting worse. What do we do? Tell me the answer. The trouble is, there has not in history ever been any answer other than, Get to work on it.

There are a thousand different ways of getting to work on it. For one thing, there's no "it." There's lots of different things. You can think of long-term goals and visions you have in mind, but even if that's what you're focused on, you're going to have to take steps towards them. The steps can be in all kinds of directions, from caring about starving children in Central America or Africa, to working on the rights of working people here, to worrying about the fact that the environment's in serious danger. There's no one thing that's the right thing to do. It depends on what your interests are and what's going on and what the problems are and so on. And you have to deal with them. There's very little that anybody can do about these things alone. Occasionally somebody can, but it's marginal. Mainly you work with other people to try to develop ideas and learn more about it and figure out appropriate tactics for the situation in question and deal with them and try to develop more support. That's the way everything happens, whether it's small changes or huge changes.

If there is a magic answer, I don't know it. But it sounds to me as if the tone of the questions and part of the disparity between listening and acting suggests—I'm sure this is unfair—Tell me something that's going to work pretty soon or else I'm not going to bother, because I've got other things to do. Nothing is going to work pretty soon, at least if it's worth doing, nor has that ever been the case.

To get back to the point, even in talks like these, the organizers told me they did get a fair amount of apparent engagement. People would ask, Can I join your group? or What can I do? or Do you have some suggestions? If that works, okay, it's fine. But usually, there's a kind of chasm between the scale of the audience, and even its immediate reaction, and the follow-up. That's depressing.

DB *You continue to be in tremendous demand for these speaking engagements. Are you considering stopping?*

I would be delighted to stop. For me it's not a great joy, frankly. I do it because I like to do it. You meet wonderful people and they're doing terrific things. It's the most important thing I can imagine doing. But if the world would go away, I'd be happy to stop. What ought to be happening is that a lot of younger people ought to be coming along and doing all these things. If that happens, fine. I'm glad to drift off into the background. That's fine by me. It's not happening much. That's another thing that I worry about. There's a real invisibility of left intellectuals who might get involved. I'm not talking about people who want to come by and say, okay, I'm your leader. Follow me. I'll run your affairs. There's always plenty of those people around. But the kind of people who are just always doing things, like whether it was workers' education or being in the streets or being around where there's something they can contribute, helping organizing—that's always been part of the vocation of intellectuals from Russell and Dewey on to people whose names you never heard of but who are doing important things. There's a visible gap there today, for all kinds of reasons. A number of people involved in these things have been talking about it. I'm sure you've heard of others.

DB *I wouldn't entirely agree. There are some voices out there, like Holly Sklar, Winona LaDuke, and others that represent a younger generation.*

It's not zero. But I think it's nothing like the scale of what it ought to be or indeed has been in the past. Maybe it was that way in the past for not great reasons. A lot of those people were around the periphery of, say, the Communist Party, which had its own serious problems. But whatever the reasons, I think there's a very detectable fact. There's plenty of left intellectuals. They're just doing other things. Most of those things are not related to, are sometimes even subversive to these kinds of activities.

DB *A talk you gave in Martha's Vineyard in late August on corporate power was broadcast on C-SPAN a couple of weeks ago. What's been the response to that?*

The usual. There's a huge flood of letters which I'm trying to answer, slowly. Many of them are mixed. Many of them are very engaged, very concerned. People say, It's terrible. I'm glad somebody's talking about it. I think the same way. What can I do, very often. There's a strange fringe. A fair number of people interpret me as saying things that are very remote from what I mean. I'll get a very enthusiastic letter saying this is great, I'm so glad to hear it, marvelous and wonderful, thanks, etc. I'd like to share with you what I've done about this. Then comes some document which is in my view often off the wall, but anyway completely unrelated to anything I'm talking about. So somewhere we're not connecting. I think I even sort of know why. There's a strange cultural phenomenon going on. It's connected with this enormous growth of cultism, irrationality, dissociation, separateness, and isolation. All of this is going together. I think another aspect is the way the population is reacting to what's happening to them. By margins that are by now so overwhelming that it's even front-page news, people are strenuously opposed to everything that's going on and are frightened and angry and are reacting like punch-drunk fighters. They're just too alone, both in their personal lives and associations and also intellectually, without anything to grasp. They don't know how to respond except in irrational ways. In some ways it has sort of the tone of a devastated peasant society after a plague swept it or an army went through and ruined everything. People have just dissolved into inability to respond.

It's kind of dramatic when you take, say, the opposite extreme in the hemisphere: Haiti. Here's the poorest country in the hemisphere. It's suffered enormous terror. People live in complete misery. I've seen a lot of Third World poverty, but it's pretty hard to match what you find in the marketplaces in Port-au-Prince, let alone the hills. Here you have the worst conceivable situation, unimaginably horrible conditions. Poor people, people in the slums, peasants in the hills, managed to create out of their own activity a very lively, vibrant civil society with grassroots movements and associations and unions and ideas and commitment and hope and enthusiasm and so on which was astonishing in scale, so much so that without any resources they were able to take over the political system. Of course it's Haiti, so the next thing that comes is the hammer on your head, which we sort of help to wield, but that's another story. However, even after it all, apparently, it still survives. That's under the worst imaginable conditions.

Then you come to the U.S., the best imaginable conditions, and people simply haven't a clue as to how to respond. The idea that we have to go to Haiti to teach them about democracy ought to have everyone in stitches. We ought to go *there* and learn something about democracy. People are asking the question here, What do I do? Go ask some illiterate Haitian peasant. They seem to know what to do. That's what you should do.

There's another aspect to this, another question that's pretty common. I commonly say, and I believe, that this is a very free society, at least for people who are relatively privileged, which is an enormous number of people. The capacity of the government to coerce is very slight. A very common response (I heard it any number of times on this latest tour, but elsewhere as well) is, What about Kent State? Incidentally, not Jackson State. That rarely comes up. What about Joe

McCarthy? Even that doesn't get mentioned because that wouldn't be relevant. I said "relatively privileged people." If you're a black organizer in the slums, sure, you have a lot of problems. But most of us aren't. Anyhow, the sense that there is repression here is enormous. In comparison, I was in Haiti briefly right at the height of the terror, and people were scared out of their wits, and rightly, but they didn't feel they had to stop because maybe someday there would be repression. If you compare the amount of repression that there is here with what there is in most of the world, where people don't even think about it—they just continue—it's pretty shocking.

DB *So that perception of omnipotent government power, do you attribute that to propaganda?*

In a very broad sense I'd attribute it to propaganda, but here you have to take the term "propaganda" pretty broadly. The whole doctrinal system, including the entertainment industry, the corporate media, the educational system, the political system, and everything else, there's a public relations industry and a huge system that has been devoting itself for a long time very intensively and even self-consciously since the Second World War towards several tasks. One of them is demonizing unions. Another is making people hate and fear the government, which you might think is a little contradictory, since they control the government. But it's not. There are plenty of things wrong with the government. But that's not what they're worried about. What they're worried about is the one thing that's right about it, namely, it's potentially influenceable by the population.

That's not true of private tyrannies. General Electric is not influenceable by the population except very indirectly through regulatory mechanisms which are very weak and which they mostly control anyhow. But you can't vote to decide what they ought to do, and you can't participate in those decisions. Those are tyrannies. Imagine yourself in the office of a public relations firm trying to turn people into the ideal state, namely manipulable atoms of consumption who are going to devote their energies to buying things that they don't want because you tell them that's what they want—advertising. They're never going to get together to challenge anything, and they won't have a thought in their heads except doing what they're told. A perfect utopia. Suppose you're trying to do that. What you do is get them to hate and fear the government, fear the bigness of the government. But not look at the Fortune 500, nor even medium-sized businesses, not ask how they work, not ask what were truisms to important mainstream political economists like Robert Brady sixty years ago, and in fact to the working-class movement throughout its history. These things are just tyrannical, totalitarian systems. You don't want people to see that. You want them to worry about the one thing that they might get involved in and that might even protect them from the depredations of private power. What would make sense would be to develop a mood of anti-politics. And it's worked. People hate the government, fear the government, are worried about the bureaucrats.

Take, say, health. A lot of concern that government bureaucrats will be controlling it. There are many more bureaucrats in insurance offices controlling you. But that's not what people worry about. It's not those pointy-headed bureaucrats in insurance offices who are making us fill out these forms and telling us what to do and we've got to pay for their lunches and their advertising while they propagandize us. That's not what people's anger and fear is focused on. What it's focused on, through very conscious manipulation and perfectly rational design, is this dangerous federal bureaucracy.

Actually, what's going on now with the attempt at devolution, reducing decision making to the state level—that makes great sense if you believe in tyranny. There are circumstances in which regionalization would be a very good move. Devolution, lowering the level of power and decisionmaking closer to the popular level, could be a step toward democracy, but not when you've got private tyrannies around. When you've got private tyrannies around, the only institution that at least in part reflects public involvement, that can cope with them, is a very powerful one, namely, the federal government. Let's say you send block grants down to the state. That's a way of guaranteeing that they're not going to get to poor people. Any even middle-sized business has all kinds of ways of pressuring states to make sure that that money ends up in their pockets and not in the pockets of hungry children. People can do this through regressive fiscal measures, the whole range of subsidies that governmental institutions provide to private powers that can threaten them—I'll move to Tennessee tomorrow—so sure, devolution under these circumstances is a great way to increase tyranny and to decrease the threat of democracy as well as to shift resources even more dramatically toward the rich and away from the poor. That's the obvious consequence of devolution. But I've never seen it discussed in the mainstream, although it's the obvious point.

What's discussed is complete irrelevancies, like whether we can trust the governors to care for the poor. What's that got to do with anything? It's totally meaningless. But that kind of absurdity is what's discussed, but not the obvious, overwhelming fact that distributing governmental resources to the lower levels will simply make them more susceptible to influence and control by private power. That's the major fact. And it's part of the same anti-politics. We want to weaken the federal government.

Incidentally, that's only half true. The federal government is not being weakened. It's just being changed. The security system is going up, not only the Pentagon, but even the internal security system, jails, etc. That aspect of the government is going up. That's not just for control, although it's partly for that. It's also because it's part of the way of transferring resources to the rich, which is virtually never discussed. In fact, it's almost off the agenda, unless you read the business press. But it's overwhelmingly significant. It ought to be a front-page article every day. By now it is so obvious it's hard to miss. The Russians are gone. The Pentagon stays the same, in fact it's even going up. We were told for fifty years, which of course was always ridiculous, that we need this huge military to defend us from the Russians. How stupid can you be, and how indoctrinated can you be? Don't you ever ask a question about what happened? What happened is, it's there for the same reason it always was. How else are Newt Gingrich's rich constituents going to stay rich? You obviously can't subject them to market discipline. They'll be out selling rags. They wouldn't know what it means to exist in a market. What they know is, the government puts money in their pockets, and the main way it does it is through the whole Pentagon system. In fact, the criminal security system is beginning to take on this character. It's reached, if not the scale of the Pentagon, it's reached a sufficient scale so that the big investment firms and even high-tech industry, defense industry, are getting intrigued by the prospects of feeding at another public cash cow. That's going up. So it's not that the government is getting weaker.

But this long and very successful effort over many, many years to get people to focus their fears and angers and hatred on the government has had its effect. We all know there's plenty to be upset about there. The primary thing to be upset about is that it is not under popular influence. It is under the influence of the private powers. That's the primary source of things we ought to worry about. But then to deal with that by giving private, unaccountable power even more power is just beyond absurdity. It's a real achievement of doctrinal managers to have been able to carry this off.

DB *You'll recall Orwell's* Animal Farm*: Two feet bad, four feet good. Public sector bad, private sector good. It's kind of playing out right now.*

It's kind of intriguing. Economists know that this is mostly nonsense. But they don't talk about it, except to each other. If you really look at the mantras, take, say, "Public sector bad." What does that mean? Is there some evidence that privatization is a good idea? It's just something you repeat because it's drilled into your head. Sure, privatization makes things more efficient. Does it? There are experiences. For example, we can look at Mexico. What privatization did was rapidly increase the number of millionaires, accelerate the decline of real wages and social conditions. Did it make things better? Well, yes, for 24 billionaires. You can object and say, That's Mexico, a corrupt Third World country. So let's take England, which is a couple of steps ahead of us in privatization. Under Thatcher they privatized the water system. It was a public utility. So now it's private. What's happened? You can even read about it on the front page of the *Financial Times*. You don't have to go to obscure publications any more. And they're pretty irate. What happened is, profits have gone through the roof, prices have gone way up, and service has gone way down. In fact, sooner or later, it's not very far from now you'll be hearing proposals from the private owners that it's not cost-effective to deliver water to scattered or small communities. What they ought to do is go to a pump in the center of town and pick it up with buckets because any smart economist can prove that that's more cost-effective and improves the GNP and that's the best distribution of resources. Sure, that's privatization.

And, not for obscure reasons, a private corporation is not in the business of being humanitarian. It's in the business of increasing profit and market share. Doing that typically is extremely harmful to the general population. It may make some numbers look good. It may create what's called an "economic miracle," meaning great for investors and murderous for the population. But there's no reason to think it's a good thing. What's claimed is, look at the inefficiency and corruption of the public institutions, which is true. Are the private ones better? The evidence for this is, as far as I know, nonexistent. What can be pointed out, and it's correct, is that public industrial systems, like the Brazilian steel industry, often lost money. But that loss of money was part of a way of subsidizing private industry. So if you keep steel prices artificially low, that will be a gain for the people who are using steel, even though that system will run at a loss.

On the other hand, if you think about the effect over the whole economy, it's much more complicated a story, and I don't think there's any single answer to it. Sometimes private industry has been efficient, and sometimes even helpful to people, which is quite different from being inefficient, in fact often unrelated to it. Sometimes it has, and many times it hasn't. It depends on the circumstances, on factors that people don't understand very well. But the idea that somehow privatization automatically improves things is absurd.

DB *In Australia earlier this year you commented that you felt like you were in somewhat of an odd situation in terms of your own political philosophy. You are defending the notion of the state and the role of the state, that the state has an active role to play to protect people's interests.*

This was actually an address at an anarchist conference. I pointed out what I think is true, that your goals and your visions are often in direct conflict. Visions are long-term things, what you'd like to achieve down the road. But if we mean by goals that which we're trying to do tomorrow, they can often appear to be in conflict with long-term visions. It's not really a conflict. I think we're in such a case right now. In the long term I think the centralized political power ought to be eliminated and dissolved and turned down ultimately to the local level, finally, with federalism and associations and so on. Sure, in the long term that's my vision. On the other hand, right now I'd like to strengthen the federal government. The reason is, we live in this world, not some other world. And in this world there happen to be huge concentrations of private power which are as close to tyranny and as close to totalitarian as anything humans have devised, and they have extraordinary power. They are unaccountable to the public.

There's only one way of defending rights that have been attained or extending their scope in the face of these private powers, and that's to maintain the one form of illegitimate power that happens to be somewhat responsive to the public and which the public can indeed influence. So you end up supporting centralized state power even though you oppose it. People who think there is a contradiction in that just aren't thinking very clearly.

DB *There are two visions of the role of government. James Madison in 1787 saw its role as "to protect the minority of the opulent against the majority." Then you have FDR in 1937 saying, "The test of our nation's progress is not whether we add more to the abundance of those who have much. It is whether we provide enough for those who have little." Obviously one of those visions is dominant today. Why?*

In the case of Madison, you have to be a little more careful. That was indeed Madison's main theme, and that's what you ought to learn in elementary school, because that in fact won. The Constitution was framed in Madisonian terms. He had a more complex argument. He was strongly opposed to democracy and warned against it. He talked about England, which was the model of the day, and said, If those guys had democracy over there the people would get together and take over the estates of the landed proprietors, and use their property for themselves instead of allowing the rich and powerful to maintain it. So obviously we can't have democracy. We don't want anything like that to happen here. So democracy is a bad thing. The prime responsibility of government is to protect the minority of the opulent against the majority, and we have to set up the constitutional system so that this will work.

But there's a hidden theme there. The hidden theme is that he is pre-capitalist. Capitalism was just in its early origins, and he was basically opposed to it. His idea was that the opulent minority are going to be benevolent aristocrats, Enlightenment gentlemen who sit around reading philosophy and who are genuine conservatives in an old-fashioned sense, a sense which doesn't exist in the U.S.: Conservatives in the European sense, who would be enlightened and benevolent. So they'll be like benevolent tyrants. So that's not inconsistent with what Roosevelt was saying, except with regard to the institutional structure.

Madison also quickly learned that that's not the case. A couple of years later he was bitterly condemning the system that he had created and talking about the "daring depravity of the times" as the rising class of business people become the "tools and tyrants" of government, overwhelming it with their force and benefiting from its gifts. That's a pretty good description of what's going on today. That was in the 1790s. When he saw that the minority of the opulent are not nice gentlemanly aristocrats or Enlightenment philosophers who are going to make sure that everybody is healthy and happy, he was outraged and infuriated. Nevertheless, the picture he presented, extricated from the context in which he understood it, has been the dominant view and now has reached an overwhelming level.

It's not anything new, incidentally. The 1920s were not all that different. A century ago was not all that different.

DB *Isn't it true that one of the tenets of classical conservative economics and philosophy is an antipathy toward concentration of power, toward monopoly? Yet these "Contractors," if you will, who call themselves conservatives, are advocating policies that are accelerating concentration.*

What we call conservatism, what used to be called liberalism—the terms are confusing—but classical liberalism was strongly opposed to concentration of power. Not what we call liberalism. It's what today we call conservatism. The terms have totally shifted in meaning, if they ever had any. The views of, say, Adam Smith and Thomas Jefferson, the intellectual founders of what people pay homage to but don't understand or choose not to understand, those people were certainly opposed to concentration of power. And it's true that the people who call themselves, say, libertarians today, whatever they may have in their minds, they are in fact advocating extreme concentration of power, in fact they're advocating some of the most totalitarian systems that humans have ever suffered under. That's not their intent, of course. But if you read Adam Smith, part of his argument for the market was that it would lead to perfect equality, equality of condition, not just equality of opportunity. Like Madison, he was a pre-capitalist and anti-capitalist person with roots in the Enlightenment and had a very different vision of the way things ought to work out. You can ask whether his argument was very good. We really don't know, experimentally, because his argument was that under conditions of perfect liberty a market would lead to equality of condition and of course we don't remotely approach that. But that aside, whatever you think about the intellectual character of his argument, it's clear what the goal was. And yes, the classical liberals, the Jeffersons and the Smiths, were opposing the concentrations of power that they saw around them, like the feudal system and the Church and royalty. They thought that ought to be dissolved. They didn't see other forms of concentration of power which only developed later. When they did see them, they didn't like them. Jefferson was a good example. He was strongly opposed to the concentrations of power that he saw developing, and warned that the banking institutions and the industrial corporations which were barely coming into existence in his day would destroy the achievements of the Revolution. As I mentioned, Madison within a few years was already having very strongly stated second thoughts about what he had framed and created.

Here there are illusions that have to be dismantled from beginning to end. Take, say, David Ricardo, who actually is much more the godfather of contemporary neoliberal economics than Adam Smith, who was a pre-capitalist. Take a look at his famous law of comparative advantage, which we're supposed to worship. It sort of works on his assumptions, but his assumptions are that capital would be pretty much immobile, partly because capital was land and land can't be moved, but partly for other reasons. He thought capital would be relatively immobile because capitalists are nice human beings and they care about the people around them, so they're not going to move their capital across the world because that would harm the people in their community and their country and naturally they have a lot of concern for them. Again, that's a pre-capitalist thought. Within capitalist ideology, that's a monstrosity. You're not supposed to care about anything except maximizing your own wealth. So Ricardo in the early nineteenth century was reflecting the residue of the pre-capitalist era, in part at least, although he's an interesting mixture.

All of the humane Enlightenment aspects of this have been eliminated, and rightly, because the logic of the capitalist enterprise is, You should not have human feelings. You should just be trying to maximize your own wealth and power. On the one hand, the idea that capitalist entrepreneurs ever thought they should be subjected to market discipline is ridiculous. You use state power as much as you can. This is again something known to economic historians, but they don't really look at it in a comprehensive way. So, for example, there are good studies showing very persuasively that, say, in the history of the U.S. that its economic growth was very closely correlated with its extremely high level of protectionism. Its biggest growth period in the late nineteenth century was a period in which tariffs here were five or ten times as high as in most of Europe, and that was great for the U.S. economy. That's very general for every developed society.

On the other hand, that very much understates the case, because there are other things you don't look at if you're an economist. It's somebody else's field. For example, one reason why the Industrial Revolution was able to be so successful in England and the U.S. was because of cheap cotton. What made cotton cheap? Extermination or elimination of the native population and bringing in slaves. That's a rather serious government intervention in the market, more than a slight market distortion. But that doesn't count. And the same economic historians will accept all sorts of myths about how developed countries used state intervention. They say that protectionism stopped in the U.S. after 1945, when the U.S. turned toward liberal internationalism. There was indeed pressure to lower tariffs. For one thing, it's not quite true that protectionism stopped. The Reaganites virtually doubled one or another form of protection.

But even if we were to agree protectionism didn't stop, it would be largely beside the point, because there was another form of state intervention in the economy, a massive form that developed at that point, but that's not the topic of economists, namely, the whole Pentagon system, which has overwhelmingly been a way of funneling public resources to advanced sectors of industry, and in fact was largely designed for that purpose. That they talk about in some other department.

If you put all these things together, you find that the doctrines of the market are mainly weapons to beat people over the head with. We don't use them ourselves. And when you actually look at the founders, they had all sorts of different ideas on the market. They were coming out of a truly conservative tradition, one that we don't have, which was rooted in the Enlightenment and existing institutions and was concerned with things like sympathy and solidarity and benevolent care, a lot of it very autocratic. That's all dissolved under the impact of a sort of hypocritical capitalist ideology which means capitalism for you, but protection for me.

DB *You've made a bit of a name for yourself in the field of linguis tics and language. It's interesting, in the current political scene, how muc the passive voice is used. There's an article on income inequality in the* Ne Yorker *(October 16), for example, which is replete with this. Inequalit happens. There's no agency. There's no active voice. People are gettir poorer. No one is making them poor. It just happens.*

Or "people were killed," not "we're killing them." That absolutely standard. In fact, that's the beautiful thing about the pas sive voice and other such devices. It makes it look as if things happe without an agent, and that's very useful when the agent shouldn't b identified because it's too close to home. Virtually all discussions o aggression and terror take place in this framework. But you're right now the idea is, something strange is just happening to the economy, which is forcing inequality. Maybe automation or trade. Nobody really knows. We can't do anything about it.

But these are social decisions. They're very easy to trace. You know who's making the decisions and why. Not exactly, but certainly to a very substantial extent we know why these things are happening. You can identify the factors in them. You can see that they are by no means inevitable. There are people who are saying very sensible things about automation and the end of work. And there's a real problem. People aren't going to get jobs because maybe someday robots will do their work. While I agree with that if you put extremely narrow bounds on the discussion, in a general sense it's completely untrue. Take a walk through Boston or any other city and see if you don't see things around where there's work to be done. Then take a look at those people over there who are idle and say, Wouldn't they like to do the work? The answer is yes to both. There is tons of work to be done, and lots of people who would like to do the work. It's just that the economic system is such a grotesque catastrophe that it can't even put together idle hands and needed work, which would be satisfying to the people and which would be beneficial to all of us. That's just the mark of a failed system. The most dramatic mark of it. Work is not something that you should try to escape from, or that ordinary human beings would want to escape from. It's something you want to do because it's fulfilling, it's creative. There's plenty of it around. It's not being done because of the extreme inadequacies of the socioeconomic system.

DB *In a recent* Covert Action Quarterly *article you wrote that "The terms of political discourse have been virtually deprived of meaning." We've talked about "conservative," for example. How can it be recovered? Is it something desirable?*

Oh, sure. Evacuation of content from the terms of discourse is a very useful device for dumbing people down. If it's impossible to talk about anything, then you've got them under control. There are things that we ought to be able to talk about in ordinary, simple words. There's nothing terribly profound here, as far as I know. If there is, nobody has discovered it. We ought to be able to talk about these things in simple, straightforward words and sentences without evasion and without going to some expert to try to make it look complicated for some other reason. I'm not recommending anti-intellectualism. There are things to learn, and they're worth learning, but the topics we are now discussing are not quantum physics. Anybody who's interested can find out about them and understand them, as much as is necessary for rational behavior in structures where you can make important decisions for yourself. We ought to try to protect substantive discourse from the attacks on it from all sides. A lot of it is from the left, I should say. One aspect of this is to protect sensible discussion from anything that has the prefix "post-" in it.

DB *In that same article, you write about the "acceleration of the deliberate policy of driving the country toward a Third World model, with sectors of great privilege, growing numbers of people sinking into poverty or real misery, and a superfluous population confined in slums or expelled to the rapidly expanding prison system." I think that's a fair summary of the current situation, but aren't the social policies that are producing those conditions a recipe for revolt and upheaval?*

Sometimes they have been, sometimes they haven't been. Slave societies can exist for a long time. It's not that it hasn't been tried before in industrial countries. Take, say, England right around the time of Ricardo, in the 1820s, when a system very much like the one they're trying to impose now was indeed imposed for the first time in an industrial country. The rulers got their way. They won political power in the mid-1830s and pretty soon they instituted the program they wanted, which was not all that different (though in a different world, of course) from what is being preached today. There were problems. The British army was spending most of its time putting down riots. Pretty soon organizing began, the Chartist movement began, labor organizing began.

By the mid-nineteenth century, the classical economists who had been deriding the idea of helping people because to help people harms them, had changed their position. You read people like, say, Nassau Senior, one of the old hawks of political economy. He was shifting towards saying, There's something to all this stuff. Then you get to John Stuart Mill in 1848 or so. That's the foundation of the modern welfare state. For a long time laissez-faire was a bad word. Why? Because, to put it in a simple formula, the rich and powerful and their intellectuals, the economists, were telling people, You don't have a right to live. You have a right to what you gain in the marketplace, but you don't have any other right to live, and any effort to help you is going to hurt you. Pretty soon these strange people got the idea, We might not have a right to live, by your lights, but you don't have a right to rule. So we're just going to take it over and kick you out. That's a little too far. The science, as it was called and still is called, was a very pliable one. Ricardo had compared the science of economics to Newton's laws, but it turned out it wasn't quite like that. When it became not usable as an instrument of class war, it simply changed. All of a sudden it turned out, Sure, you have a right to live and we have to adjust to your demands, because otherwise we're not going to have a right to rule.

Exactly what form that organizing will take now ... it's already taken some form. It happens to be taking very antisocial forms. But that is a reflection of social and cultural factors in the society. It doesn't have to. As I mentioned before, you go to the opposite extreme in our hemisphere, to Haiti, where it took very constructive forms. So if it doesn't take constructive forms here, that's our fault. We have no one to blame but ourselves.

DB *But let's say you're a CEO of a major corporation. Isn't it in your economic interest to keep enough change in my pocket so that I'll buy your products?*

That's an interesting question, and nobody knows the answer to it. It was a question that had an answer in a national economy. So if you go back to the 1920s, at the time of the big automobile manufacturing burst, that was the question that Henry Ford raised. He drew the conclusion that you just drew. He said, I'd better give these guys a decent wage or nobody's going to buy my cars. So he raised workers' salaries beyond what he was forced to by market pressures. And others went along. That was on the reasoning that you just outlined, and it made sort of sense in a national economy.

Does it make sense in an international economy? Does it make sense in an international economy where you can shift production to the poorest and most deprived and most depressed regions where you have security forces keeping people under control and you don't have to worry about environmental conditions and you have plenty of women pouring off the farms to work under impossible conditions and get burnt to death in factory fires and die from overwork and somebody else replaces them and that production is then integrated through the global system so that value is added where you have skilled workers and maybe pay a little more but you don't have many of them? Finally it's sold to the rich people in all the societies. Even the poorest Third World country has a very rich elite. As you take this kind of structural Third World model and transfer it over to the rich countries—it's a structural model, it's not in absolute terms—they have a sector of consumers that's not trivial. Even if there's plenty of superfluous people and huge numbers in jail and a lot of people suffering or even starving. So the question is, Can that work? As a technical question, nobody really knows the answer. And it doesn't make any difference anyway. We shouldn't even be allowing ourselves to ask it. The point is that whether it could work or not, it's a total monstrosity. Fascism works, too. In fact, it worked rather well from an economic point of view. It was quite successful. That doesn't mean it's not a monstrosity. So there is the technical question, Will it work? To that nobody knows the answer. But there's also a human question of whether we should even ask, and the answer to that is, Of course not. That's not the CEO's question, but it should be everybody else's.

DB *What about the issue of the debt as a tactic of imposing a kind of de facto structural adjustment in the U.S.?*

There's a lot to say about it. Basically, yes. What is being said about the debt is for the most part nonsense. The one thing that is correct, which is hidden there, is that it is a weapon for cutting back social spending. In fact, it very likely was created for that reason. Most of the debt is Reagan debt. If you look back, it's clear at the time, and I think it's becoming clearer and clearer, that their borrow-and-spend lunacy which did substantially increase the debt, like 80% as compared with that accumulated over a couple hundred years, was conceived of and is now being very efficiently used as a weapon to cut back those parts of government that help the general population, while incidentally increasing spending for those parts of the government that help the very rich, like the Pentagon system.

***

November 3, 1995

DB *To pick up where we left off the other day, maybe we should make a distinction between what is called "the debt" and the deficit.*

It's just a technical difference. The deficit is a year-by-year accounting of the ratio between income and outgo in each year. The debt is what's accumulated over time. So if the deficit stays high, the debt will continue to grow. If the deficit can be negative, then the debt cuts down.

DB *You mentioned that a lot is left out in the discussion about the debt. Like what?*

I should say it's not left out by serious professional economists who write about it, like Robert Eisner, who has done some of the best work. But it's left out of the public debate. One point is that the debt, though high (and it certainly grew substantially during the Reagan years), nevertheless is not high by either comparative or historical standards. So in the past it has often been higher, and in other countries it's higher. "High" means relative to the total economy, GNP or GDP, whatever you decide to measure. Relative to that, it's not high.

The second point is that a debt is just part of living. There isn't a business around that isn't in debt. You borrow for, say, capital investment. Every person is in debt, virtually, unless they hide their money under the mattress. Almost everyone who has a car or a home or is sending their kids to college or doing anything is in debt. There's nothing wrong with that. If you weren't, you wouldn't have a home or a car or a television set. You wouldn't be able to buy things on your MasterCard. Your kids wouldn't go to college. Debt is just the way the system functions.

A third point is that the calculations for the federal government don't make any sense because they don't distinguish between that part of the debt that is for capital investment, and therefore contributes to economic growth and in fact further income for the government and everybody else, and that part of the debt which is just operating expenses. Every business makes that distinction. Most of the states make that distinction. Unless you make that distinction you're just in a dream world.

So, to begin with, the whole thing is off the mark from the start. If you ask about debt, the question to ask is, What's it for? Take a family. If you go to Las Vegas and spend all your money and end up in debt and then you use the debt for more going to Las Vegas, that's a bad use of debt. If you use the same amount of borrowing for a house or a car or your children's education or putting into a business or buying books, then it could be a fine debt, in fact very constructive. In fact, forgetting what it does for you as a person, keeping to the strictest, narrowest economic considerations, it can contribute to further income. That's exactly why businesses go into debt and people go into debt. One of the reasons. For a business it's about the only reason. For people there are lots of good reasons.

When you turn to the government, you have to ask the same question: What's the borrowing for? If the point of the borrowing is to put a lot of money into the pockets of Newt Gingrich's rich constituents, which is in fact what it's for, it's like going to Las Vegas and wasting your money. On the other hand, if the same debt is used to improve what's called human capital, that means to help children be healthier, better educated, more skilled, and so on—you have to put everything in terms of the word "capital" to be serious, although it's not serious. It's called "human capital." It's part of our kind of insane ideology. So if it's used for human capital, by any measure it's a wise debt. For example, it will increase economic growth, because improving human capital is one of the standard ways—the World Bank will tell you this—for increasing economic growth. What is going to determine much of the quality of life a little bit down the road—say you're worried about your children—is how the economy's working. That will determine a large part of what their lives are going to be like. It's not the only thing, again, but let's keep to that. That will depend on things like whether there is an educated, healthy, skilled population capable of increasing productivity and doing useful things, whether there's a livable environment, so you're not falling on the floor and dying because of pollution. Whether there's infrastructure, like can you get to work without spending three hours in a traffic jam, are there schools, are there hospitals—all of that is what contributes to economic growth in the narrowest terms.

Incidentally, relative equality also contributes to economic growth. Not too much is understood about these problems. Take the World Bank. Go out to the limits. They recognize that one of the factors, probably the major factor, that led to East Asian growth is relative equality, high infrastructure spending, investment in education, all of these things. It's kind of common sense, and it's shown by history. So if public spending is used for those purposes, then it contributes to the welfare of future generations, and then the debt is very wise, in fact it's contributing to growth.

This idea that we're somehow putting a burden on future generations by the debt is another small fraud. The debt is mostly owned by Americans. The latest figures I've seen show about 80% owned by Americans, which means that paying the debt goes back into the pockets of American citizens. You could claim that it has a very negative redistributive effect. That's probably true. I don't know if anybody knows the numbers, but it stands to reason that the people who own Treasury securities are not cab drivers. So the debt is by and large like other forms of social policy, that is, a technique by which the poor pay off the rich. But that's internal to the country. It's not a matter of putting a burden on your children, except in the sense that the whole regressive system puts a burden on your children because they're going to be doing all sorts of things to pay off the rich. The debt is another one. But the Gingrich line about how you've got to save future generations is not only ridiculous, but it's the opposite of the truth. By cutting back the kinds of government spending they want cut back, they're cutting back future economic growth and making life worse for the next generation, for just the reasons I mentioned.

These are things which certainly have to be seriously taken into consideration when you talk about the debt and the annual deficit.

Another factor has to do with what the public thinks of all of this. Business is totally in favor of cutting it back. There's overwhelming support for it, even those parts of business that will be harmed by it. That's kind of interesting. Because apparently for them, the class interest is overwhelming the immediate profit interest. So the class interest of rolling back all the social programs and ensuring that the government works only for the rich and destroying the regulatory apparatus and improving the options for corporate crime, which is what changing the tort system and the regulatory system means, all of that is so overwhelmingly beneficial that they're willing to face the costs, to some extent, of less government service for the rich.

I should say only to some extent. If you look at the National Association of Manufacturers, they're calling for more government assistance for, say, export promotion, meaning put money in their pockets. Newt Gingrich is not calling for cutting down the Pentagon system, putting money in the pockets of his rich constituents and others like them. On the contrary. Gingrich and the Heritage Foundation want a much bigger nanny state for the rich. So it's mixed. But they're willing to do things even that might harm profit because of the overwhelming advantages of destroying a whole system which is preventing them from robbing everybody blind. So that's something.

So the business community is for it. Read *Business Week*. It's uniform. In the political system, the leadership of both parties (not the scattered dissidents) is virtually 100% for it. So when Clinton goes on the radio to criticize the Republican budget program, he says, Of course we must balance the budget and eliminate the debt. That's not even in question.

But there's another segment of the country, namely, the population. There are polls. There was recently a poll asking what people thought the primary issue was in the country. 5% said the debt. 5% said homelessness. So the number of people who think it's the prime issue is the same as the number of people who think it's homelessness. That shows you how people rank it. When asked, Should we eliminate the debt, here the polls are very carefully crafted. There are two sets of questions, one for headline writers and NPR and a set of questions for people who want to know the answers. The questions for the headline writers are, Would you like to see the debt eliminated? Most people say, Yes. It's like asking, Would you like your mortgage eliminated? That's for the headlines: Americans Voted for Balanced Budget.

Everybody Wants the Debt Eliminated. Americans Like the GOP Agenda, etc. Then comes the question that matters: Do you want the debt eliminated or the deficit reduced at the cost of ______. Then come a lot of "of's": cutback in health care, environmental protection, education. Then it goes way down. Depending on how the question is framed, it goes down to roughly 25% thinking it should be done at all, let alone thinking it's a high priority. It's like asking the question, Do you want your mortgage eliminated at the cost of giving up your house? You get a different answer to the question of would you like your mortgage eliminated. So this is part of the scam done by the public relations industry for the benefit of the doctrinal institutions. If you look at the bottom of the column, where the headline says Americans Want Balanced Budget, you sometimes get some of this data. So in general, the public is taking kind of a realistic attitude. They don't think it's that important, it's about at the level of homelessness, and they don't want it to happen at the cost that it's going to take.

Suppose you raised the serious question and said, Do you want the debt reduced at the cost of the health and welfare and economic growth of the next generation? Because that's what it means. I'm sure as soon as this is laid out you'll get overwhelming opposition, especially if it's understood exactly why this is the case.

On top of all of this, there is some historical experience. Here you have to be pretty cautious, because very little is understood about these matters, as the better economists will agree. It's very speculative. But there's some evidence. For example, there have been periods of attempts to balance the budget. I think there have been about half a dozen since the 1820s. I think every single one has led very quickly to a very serious recession or a deep depression. It's not hard to see why. If you think it through, you can see why that should be.

On the other hand, there are also rather sophisticated studies of the effect of the deficit on things like consumption, investment, growth, and so on. It tends to have a sort of positive correlation. It tends to be the case that deficits contribute to growth, consumption levels, investment, production, trade, the usual measures. These are complicated measures, and you don't want to say anything with much confidence. But it looks like that, and you can see why it would be the case.

If you did a really serious analysis, which would be extremely hard, you'd ask the same question as about a person borrowing. Do you borrow so you can gamble in Las Vegas or do you borrow for your children's education? If you could ask that question, which is sophisticated, and ask, Insofar as debt was used for productive government investment, like infrastructure, health, the environment, and so on, what was its effect? vs. debt for building the F-22, I'm pretty sure you'd get a pretty sharp answer. But that's a hard question to ask, and I don't think anybody's asked it.

In any event, if you want to rethink the question of debt, you have to start from the beginning and redo it from a totally different perspective. Again, if we had anything remotely like a free press around, these would be the front-page stories, what they'd be telling people every day. You can't claim that they don't tell you. If you really read everything, you'll find somebody saying this down on a back page or a piece of an op-ed. But what people are deluged with is a different story. Unless you carry out a research effort, it's very hard to know anything about these topics.

Interesting to me is that despite the deluge, people do not believe that the debt is an important issue. That's pretty astonishing. I don't know how long that can go on.

DB *One of the things you often do is challenge assumptions. So many things are just taken for granted, and that's what the discourse is built upon. Like, We need to have a balanced budget. But citing a recent CBS News-New York Times poll, Americans, when asked whether they would want to sustain Medicare at current levels or balance the budget, by 3 to 1 said that they would rather have Medicare. This poll, incidentally, was described by the Speaker of the House as an example of "disinformation."*

And the *Times*, which ran the poll well, for once (that was a lead front-page story) didn't mention that this has been a consistent figure all the way back. So you go back to last December. There were similar polls. Again it turns out, although the questions weren't framed exactly the same way, that when people were asked, Do you want budget balancing at the cost of medical assistance, health care, again it was about 3 to 1 opposed. So these are fairly steady figures, and it's interesting that they're holding up despite the propaganda. When people are asked, Would you like to have higher taxes for more medical research, it's about 75% in favor. I don't remember the last numbers, but quite consistently over the years the polls have indicated that people are in favor of higher taxes if they're used for things like health or education. Even foreign aid, believe it or not, if it goes to the poor. And of course, overwhelmingly the population thinks that the government has a responsibility to help the poor here.

They are also opposed to welfare, and that's a success of the propaganda system. But yes, these poll results were interesting and important, have been consistent and generalized to almost everything else. And it hasn't gone totally unnoticed. For example, Brad Knickerbocker is a well-known Washington correspondent for the *Christian Science Monitor*. He's dealing mostly with environmental and energy issues these days. He had a column in which he said, kind of quizzically, that it's almost as if Congress is looking at the polls and deciding to do the opposite. He was talking about environment and energy issues, where again it's extremely dramatic, but it generalizes across the board. I think it's hard to find a time in American history when policy has been so radically opposed to public opinion on issue after issue. It's even true on the things that are going up.

The one big thing that's going up is Pentagon spending. By about 6 to 1, the population wants it either stable or reduced. So even that is overwhelmingly opposed by the public. What you're getting in the commentary is kind of interesting. Gingrich is plainly a total cynic, but a pretty efficient one. His line, which is repeated by the Heritage Foundation and the Cato Institute, is that there's a philosophical issue. People shouldn't be compelled to pay for things they don't want, and that's why we have to cut down food for starving children. A lot of people don't want that, and our philosophy says they shouldn't have to pay for that. But somehow our philosophy says you can increase the Pentagon budget over the opposition of maybe three-quarters of the population because that puts money in my pockets. So there the philosophical issue disappears. Fortunately philosophy is a pretty subtle discipline, as we teach around here, and Gingrich understands that, along with the Heritage Foundation and the rest of the frauds who are putting forth their ridiculous distortion of libertarian philosophy.

DB *But there is a lot of confusion in the public. We talked about this the other day. There are all kinds of contradictory currents that are swirling around. For example, in a recent article you cited a poll in which about 80% of the population believes that the economic system is "inherently* *unfair," and the government is "run for the benefit of the few and the special interests, not the people." This is up from a steady 50%. But what is meant by "special interests"?*

That's a good question. I think I mentioned that in the article. I said what they mean by "special interests" is another question. But these questions have been asked for a long time in polls, a little differently worded so you get some different numbers, but for a long time about half the population was saying, when asked a bunch of open questions—like, Who do you think the government is run for? would say something like that: the few, the special interests, not the people. Now it's 82%, which is unprecedented. It means that 82% of the population don't even think we have a political system, not a small number.

What do they mean by special interests? Here you've got to start looking a little more closely. Chances are, judging by other polls and other sources of information, that if people are asked, Who are the special interests? they will probably say, welfare mothers, government bureaucrats, elitist professionals, liberals who run the media, unions. These things would be listed. How many would say, Fortune 500, I don't know. Probably not too many. We have a fantastic propaganda system in this country. There's been nothing like it in history. It's the whole public relations industry and the entertainment industry. The media, which everybody talks about, including me, are a small part of it. I talk about mostly that sector of the media that goes to a small part of the population, the educated sector. But if you look at the whole system, it's just vast. And it is dedicated to certain principles. It wants to destroy democracy. That's its main goal. That means destroy every form of organization and association that might lead to democracy. So you have to demonize unions. And you have to isolate people and atomize them and separate them and make them hate and fear one another and create illusions about where power is. A major goal of this whole doctrinal system for fifty years has been to create the mood of what is now called anti-politics.

That succeeded. People focus their anger and fear on the government, the one part of the whole system of power that they can influence, and don't much see the real systems of power, the hand that's over it, the triviality stated by John Dewey that "Politics is the shadow on society cast by big business." It ought to be a truism, but few people understand. So there's plenty of confusion. And it shows up point by point.

Take, say, unions. About 80% of the population think working people don't have enough influence on what goes on. On the other hand, a great many people think unions have too much influence. There's some truth to that. Unions don't really closely represent working people. So there's an element of truth to that. But that's not what they mean. The point is that democratic unions are the way in which working people could have more of a say in things. But that's been driven out of people's minds.

Or take, say, welfare, a dramatic case. I think the last figure I saw was 80% of the population thought that the government has a responsibility to help the poor. There is also substantial opposition to welfare, which is the government helping the poor. The reason is the Reagan fairy tales: black mothers in Cadillacs, teenaged girls having babies so that you'll pay for them, all that kind of fraud. So people are opposed to welfare. If that's welfare, why should I pay for it? I want to help the poor.

Also, people vastly overestimate the amount of money that goes to welfare. The U.S. has always had quite low social expenditures by comparative standards, and has been reducing them very sharply since 1970. For example, AFDC is now virtually wiped out, reduced by almost a half since the 1970s. This feeling that there is a huge welfare burden is a total joke. I'm not talking about the real welfare (to the rich), but that trickle of welfare that goes to people who need help, which has never been high, and it's been declining very sharply. I think about a third, a quarter of the population think it's the biggest item in the federal budget. It's almost invisible. They feel the same thing about foreign aid, which is really invisible. Again, about a quarter of the population think it's the biggest item in the federal budget. And they think they're very heavily taxed. We're low taxed. And the taxes are extremely regressive.

There are two figures that are interesting, pre-tax income and actual income post-tax and post-benefit. So if you take into account food stamps, the effect of taxes, etc., and you ask, What do people have after all that system's done?—in most countries, other countries like ours, it changes things a lot. Pre-tax inequality is not all that different in those countries from here. In the U.S., post-tax inequality, including all of these government transfers, is virtually the same as pre-tax. So the whole system of taxes and benefits doesn't change much. In most other countries it changes a lot, which is why we have twice the level of poverty of our next nearest competitor, England, and much more than most other countries. Because the whole system doesn't do much. It's a highly regressive system. If you did a serious count, which people don't do, it would be much more regressive.

Consider, for example, that a lot of things that are taxes aren't called taxes. Take, say, New York City. It has just cut down expenditures for mass transit. So that's less tax money spent. On the other hand, they raised fares, which means more taxes. Fares are just taxes by another name. There's a difference between the cuts and the taxes. The taxes are regressive. First of all, even if executives and poor people took subways to the same extent, it would be a highly regressive tax. But of course they don't. Overwhelmingly, the subways are used by the poor. So this is a radically regressive tax, and it's really socking it to people who can't pay for it and enriching the people who don't have to. If you look more closely, it's even more dramatic. For example, the state administration has given what they call "subsidies," a funny word for it, to public transportation, which means people's money is being used for themselves. But have a look at it. They've cut down quite significantly the subsidy that goes to mass public transportation, like subways and buses, and increased the amount that's going to commuter rail lines. Now they cut them both a little, but they cut the subways much more than the commuter rail lines. In fact, the costs, the last figures I saw, the state contribution to these was about ten to one in favor of commuter rail lines. Who rides commuter rail lines? Executives living out in Westchester County and Long Island. Who rides subways? People living in Queens trying to get to Brooklyn, poor kids trying to get to school. That's taxes. If anybody were to take that stuff into account, you would see that the system is ... in fact the system already is flat by economists' calculations, so to talk about a "flat tax" is a joke. That's just talking about making it more regressive. It's already more or less flat and has been, certainly, since the Reagan years. If you did a real calculation, it's not flat, because the real costs are imposed on the poor.

Take, say, Boston. I live in the suburbs, which are mostly fairly wealthy people. You go a couple of miles from here and you get to the city, which is very poor people. I drove into Boston this morning.

Who's paying for the fact that I can drive there? Who's keeping the roads up? Who's paying for the local cops? Who's paying for the services? Not the guys who live in my suburb. We just rip off the poor people. And every city works like that. It's designed in such a way that the poor pay off the rich by various techniques.

DB *And who's paying for the cheapest gasoline in the world?*

That's right.

DB *The Pentagon.*

Actually, you have to be a little careful. It's keeping the oil prices within a range. It doesn't want them to get too low or too high. Because if the prices get too low it harms the big energy companies, which are mostly U.S.-based, the ones that aren't British. And you don't want that to happen, because they're an important part of the wealthy sector. On the other hand, if it goes too high it harms other sectors of the economy. So they're always looking for it to be in a certain band. If you look at policy over the years, it's been, Not too high, not too low.

DB *There's a group here in Boston, Share the Wealth. They've been doing a lot of research and reports on the tax code. They're reporting that in the 1950s corporations paid something like 40% of all the taxes that IRS collected. In the 1990s it's down to something like a quarter of that. That might be a piece of information that would be of interest to people.*

It's not just that. Take a look at state taxes and the rest. The tax code always was regressive. We never had much of a progressive tax. Take a look at work by real analysts like Joseph Pechman and others from years and years ago. They pointed out that if you calculate everything—state taxes, sales taxes, the whole business—you get a rather flat tax. It's become much worse in the last couple of years. These are part of it. And it's getting worse. The programs that are currently on the table, which they call flat tax programs—a meaningless term because we already have a flat tax—to tilt the scale even more sharply against the poor, also include things like a cutback on capital gains taxes. Capital gains happen to be about half the income for the top one percent of the population, then tailing off very, very sharply.

That's saying, If you're in the top one percent we're going to not even tax you for half your income, which is huge. All of these are complicated devices for ensuring that the poor—like 80% of the population—pay off the rich.

You read stories, like the article you gave me the other day from the *New Yorker* by John Cassidy, about how all of this is the inexorable workings of the capitalist system. The market in its genius is having these unpleasant effects. That is simply nonsense. These are social policies. You could make the policies different.

DB *He also says it's a mystery how people are becoming poorer.*

If you look at that article, there are some very interesting internal contradictions in it. He's very critical of all these things that are happening. Isn't it sad so many people are suffering, etc. He's goodhearted. But then there's the miracle of the market, the genius of the market, the mysteries. On the other hand, when he talks about the market, he only mentions three corporations: Hughes, Grumman, and McDonnell Douglas. He says that's the way the market is functioning. *That's* the way the market is functioning? These are state-subsidized corporations. You could hardly pick better examples of state industry. The only thing that makes them part of the market is that the profits go into private pockets. But the public is paying for it. That's why those corporations function.

DB *I think it was you that told me about this issue of people's perceptions and these contradictory currents, that most Americans believe that "From each according to his ability, to each according to his need"* (Marx) *is part of the Bill of Rights.*

Part of the Constitution. That was a poll taken around 1976, the Bicentennial. There were many polls taken. Among other things, they gave people cliché-type things and said, Which do you think are in the Constitution? About 50% said that that's in the Constitution because they take it to be so obvious. It tells you something about the failure of the left to organize. If half the population assumes that the most extreme position is not only true but must even be in the Constitution, that indicates a big failure on the left.

DB *We're in the era of reform, another Orwellism, tax reform,* *welfare reform. There's also something called "lobbying reform." There's a proposal to defund the left, to curb activities by non-profit groups. It's interesting to see what groups are mentioned there as part of the left.*

Although one should be very careful about the word "reform." We don't call what Hitler did reform. Reform has a nice feel about it. It's supposed to make things better. So we should never use the word. We should talk about changes. The same with "promise." Every article you read in the paper says, You may or may not like what the Republicans are doing, but they're fulfilling their promise to the American people. If I say I'm going to beat you to a pulp, and I do it, that's not a promise. I didn't promise to do it. I threatened to do it. So what they ought to say is, The Republicans are keeping their threat to the American people. Especially when we know how the American people feel about it. These are not reforms, any more than we'd say Stalin and Hitler instituted reforms. These are changes. You can like them or dislike them, but they're not reforms.

There are two things going on that fall under what you mentioned. One is the Istook Amendment, which is working its way through. I don't think it's going to make it. It's too extreme. But it's in the legislative process now. That's a very cynical device to try to ensure that only, say, military industry and big corporations can lobby. Anyone who has any popular interest at heart can't lobby, can't try to press their interests in the public arena. The idea is to strike another massive blow at what's left of the democratic system by restricting even entry into the public arena in the form of lobbying, that is, pressing for your position. "Lobbying" means, like, writing a letter to your representative, or whatever you do. Restricting even that only to people who get huge government handouts.

The way it's done is trying various methods. The first one was to say, If you receive government funding and you're a non-profit organization, you can't use your own money for lobbying. Notice there's no issue about using federal money for lobbying. That's already illegal. So that's out of the question. The question is, can you use your own money? Suppose 5% of your money comes from a federal grant, can you use the other 95% for putting forward your interest in a cleaner environment or more health care? The first proposal was to add that condition that you can't, but of course restrict it only to nonprofit organizations. Meaning if you're making profit, like these three exemplars of the capitalist system, Hughes, McDonnell Douglas, and Grumman, then you can continue to lobby at will because you're profit-making. That got a certain amount of flak.

The later proposal, which may actually go through, is to require that nonprofit organizations provide accounting of every penny they spend on every possible thing, which will wildly increase bureaucratic costs and drive most of them out of business.

That's one aspect of it, the Istook Amendment. The other aspect is this program of defunding the left, which is itself interesting. I think it was started by the Cato Institute. It's being pushed by Congress and was reported in the *Wall Street Journal*. That's very interesting. They quote the Heritage Foundation and Gingrich as to why we've got to start defunding the left, because it's unfair for the government to be involved in pushing these political agendas.

"Agenda" is an interesting word. An agenda is something that people have who are trying to do bad things, like help poor people or clean up the environment. That's an agenda. It's not an agenda if you're trying to put more money in your pocket. So there are all these guys with agendas, and the government's funding them, and that's wrong, because why should we fund the left?

Take a look at the list. The list was right there in the *Wall Street Journal*. The main organization on the left that they had to stop funding was Catholic Relief Services, a very left-wing organization. So why do they have to defund that part of the left? They explained that there are, in fact, priests and nuns, who, for free, are working in Head Start programs and helping poor people get heating for their homes. Those are left-wing agendas. They are helping people. And since priests and nuns are working on that, and sometimes they get a little bit of government money for it, you've got to defund them. That was the main organization. The second one was the American Association of Retired Persons, the AARP. That was the second left-wing organization. They explained why they had to defund that part of the left. The reason was that AARP was running a program to try to help elderly people who are poor to get jobs. That's a left-wing agenda, so they've got to stop that. Incidentally, the *Wall Street Journal* had another article in which they said that one out of six elderly people are suffering from hunger, many actually starving. But if you're trying to get them jobs, that's a left-wing program and we have to defund it. The next was some conservation organization. By their standards, anyone who has the slightest concern for human beings is on "the left." Rather flattering, actually, and also intriguing that the mislabelled "conservatives" define themselves to include only people who would be regarded as pathologically insane by rational—and certainly by authentic conservative—standards.

DB *Even the American Heart Association, which they want to prevent from speaking out against the dangers of smoking and secondhand smoke. Meanwhile Philip Morris and the heavily subsidized tobacco industry can lobby to its heart's content.*

On the Istook Amendment, and on the whole issue, one of the biggest supporters is the alcohol industry. They're pushing it very hard. They don't want people to be able to say, There is harm in alcohol, which in fact there is, much greater than hard drugs, though not as bad as tobacco. The biggest corporate funder by far for all of these guys, including last November, was Philip Morris, which is also one of the biggest killers, so they need the protection. In fact, the agenda, if I can borrow their word, is so clear, obvious, and dramatic that it takes a real genius to miss it.

DB *Let's talk a little bit more about the media and their impact. This summer there was a spate of mega-mergers in the media. Disney took over Cap Cities/ABC. Westinghouse took over CBS. Time-Warner took over Turner. What is your assessment of these mergers?*

First of all, remember they're part of something much more general. There's a merger wave now which has no precedent. Even in the peak of the Reagan years it wasn't like this. And there's a move towards what the business press is calling "mega-corporations." Which means radically increasing the tyrannical, totalitarian structure of the global and domestic economies. These are of course tyrannies and totalitarian institutions. Nobody should have any doubt about that. As they get more powerful and integrated, they constitute in that alone a big attack on democracy and a big attack on markets, because as they dominate interactions—that means internal to these totalitarian structures—these huge command economies go way beyond anything people called, ludicrously, socialist. The media mergers are one piece of that. The big story is the increasing concentration of tyrannical power in private, unaccountable hands, which is far more important than what's happening in the media.

As to the media, what will the effect of this be? I have always been a bit of a skeptic about this. I didn't really pay a lot of attention to it. I don't think it matters a lot if, say, in Boston there are two or three corporate newspapers or one corporate newspaper. There's some difference, but not a huge difference. Say there are three channels on television which are owned by huge mega-corporations and conglomerates and then it turns out later there's only one because they're all owned by Murdoch. I suspect that the difference won't be substantial.

It will be something of a difference, because even within a system where power resides in extremely narrow hands, let's say the Politburo in Russia, if there are factions within the Politburo there's a little more freedom than if there are no factions within it. But the big point is the Politburo, not the amount of factional relations within it. Even in totalitarian states, they vary in the amount of internal factionalism within the sector that controls power. But it's the anti-democratic character of it that's significant, not the marginal question of the amount of factionalism there is. Things like the mergers of the media, what they're doing is cutting down the factionalism in the Politburo, which surely is something to worry about, but we're wasting our time if we pay too much attention to it, missing the larger picture.

Not a lot of people, including my close friends and associates, agree with me on this one, so I don't mean to say it's obvious. I suppose it's not. But that's my view.

But let me just give you a personal experience. You remember our story with Warner and the first book (*Counter-Revolutionary Violence: Bloodbaths in Fact and Propaganda*) that Ed Herman and I wrote in 1973. The publishing house, Warner Modular, that produced it was put out of business, meaning they not only destroyed our book, but they destroyed all the books that Warner Modular published. The decision to carry out this massive attack against freedom of speech was made by an executive of Warner Communications, who didn't like our book. Incidentally, none of this elicited any reaction from alleged defenders of freedom of speech (Ben Bagdikian later wrote about it). But they weren't Time-Warner in those days. It was Warner Communications. Big enough, but nowhere near what it is now and nowhere near what it is after the latest merger. Did that make a difference in the way they behave? No, not really. Marginal differences. I think the analogy would be something like factions within the Politburo.

DB *I've been talking to Bob Parry (independent journalist) and Jeff Cohen (Fairness and Accuracy in Reporting) about this. They contend that it is making a difference, the mega-mergers, the concentration, that there's more timidity—that's hard to imagine—and skittishness in the newsroom because there are fewer jobs. So you have fewer options.*

That's a different matter. I think they're confusing two different things. Even without the mergers, the jobs are going down. That's quite independent. Maybe the mergers have some effect on it, but I doubt if it's large. The major thing is that news services are going down. That makes sense, because after all the purpose of this whole system is to destroy democracy, that is, to remove people from the public arena. So the more you can put into sitcoms and advertising, and the less you put into giving them news, the better it is. You've got to give them some news. They want to have some vague idea of what's going on. But there are natural pressures within a state capitalist economy to drive out anything that might bring the population into the public arena, and news is one of those things. So of course there are going to be pressures on cutting down news, apart from the fact that news isn't terribly profitable. News is a capital-intensive operation from the point of view of the media. You're also not going to get as much advertising for it. It doesn't contribute to the needs of advertisers. So just as advertisers are unlikely to fund a documentary on saving health care, they're not going to fund a news program which is in effect a documentary by bringing some version of the facts, maybe a distorted version, to large parts of the public. It's not in their interest to do so.

Hence, independent of mergers, there's going to be continual pressure, and there is, strikingly, now, on cutting back investigative reporting. Maybe there will still be investigative reporting that keeps right to the surface, like a corrupt judge. Anything insignificant. Maybe there will be programs on the O.J. Simpson trial. Anything to keep people's minds off serious things. That could continue. And the kind of reporting that contributes to fear and hate, that will continue. But just think of the funders and ask what their interest is in presenting an honest view of the world. It's very slight. That's true whether there are mergers or not. So it may be that there's an effect, but I suspect it's a marginal effect. Incidentally, it could go the other way, too. It could turn out that if you have one totalitarian institution running all the media, they might allow more deviation internally because it's much less of a threat to them. I don't say that would happen, but it could.

Let me give you an example. I was recently in Australia, which is quite different from here. I was on Australian World Services, their version of the BBC, talking about the Timor Gap Treaty. It's a big issue in Australia. Australia was coming to the World Court, being charged with a violation of international law. I had a half-hour interview and was very critical of the Australian position. That's Australia, not the U.S. I couldn't imagine it happening here. It was on Australian World Services being beamed into Indonesia through the *Murdoch satellite*, no less.

DB *Jeff Cohen and others have commented on the surge in right-wing media, radio talk shows specifically. Rupert Murdoch has just funded* The Standard, *a new weekly right-wing journal. There's* USA Today *and on and on. You don't detect that?*

Sure. There's been a big rise in this. It's always going on, but there's an acceleration since the early 1970s. There are two things that happened. One is that the sixties frightened a lot of people, including the liberals. Terribly frightened. There was this "crisis of democracy." People were getting involved in the public arena. We've got to drive them back to their preferred apathy and ignorance. So that's across the spectrum, liberal to conservative. That led to a big attack on universities, on independent thought, on independent media, just about everything, across the spectrum. That's one thing.

The second factor was that very substantial new weapons were coming into the hands of private power around that time. There was also independently an acceleration in the globalization of the economy, telecommunications revolutions, deregulation of the financial system, all of these things were having the effect of putting very powerful weapons in private hands. So quite apart from the sixties, there would have been an effort to move from containment of New Deal-style liberalism, to rollback of it. That has happened quite dramatically.

The last liberal president in the U.S. was Richard Nixon. Ever since then it's been, starting with Carter, an attack on social programs, an increase in the regressive forms of state power like the Pentagon system. These things were simultaneous. There had been talk shows. They had been pretty awful, but there was some kind of mixture. They shifted very sharply towards the right around this point, as did everything else. So the flooding of college campuses with glossy, super-ultra-right-wing newspapers in everybody's mailbox, that started around then. The Olin professorships of free enterprise, and contributions to academic freedom of that kind, that also increased, as did the very narrowly focused right-wing foundations which are trying to destroy the educational system. They want to destroy public education. You may have noticed yesterday in Boston, Governor Weld announced what amounts to the destruction of the public education system. It sneaked into a legislative bill. All of this stuff has been going on. It's picking up, and that's what they were referring to. It's real enough, but I think it's not due to mega-mergers.

DB *We're not talking about a monolith here. You mentioned that* Wall Street Journal *article, Hunger Surges Among the Elderly. They had a piece a couple of days ago on the positive impact of government welfare programs in South Carolina. The* New York Times *is writing about class conflict. So there are some contradictory streams here as well.*

There are all sorts of contradictions. Take the cutback of the regulatory apparatus. The *Times* also had a big story a couple of weeks ago on the fact that the big investment firms are very unhappy about it. They need the Securities and Exchange Commission. A market, to the extent that it exists, is a very expensive affair. Markets cost a lot of money to set up and a lot of money to police. If you don't set them up and you don't police them there's not going to be any market. There's just going to be fraud and corruption and disaster and rapid collapses that are going to wipe things out. So the big guys, the big investment firms and financial institutions and banks, rely on the SEC as government intervention to protect the functioning of markets to the extent that they exist, which is a limited but not zero extent. And the attack on these commissions is something they're not at all happy about. The same is true of the Commerce Department. The Commerce Department is now under attack by the Republican freshmen. But big business wants it. It just puts money into their pockets. The Commerce Department is one of the welfare systems for the rich, and they don't want that to disappear.

The same is true on environmental issues. If you notice, this whole Republican freshman attack was going right after environmental issues. But they're being beaten back on that one, to a large extent because big corporations who can think five years ahead realize that they would like to have a world five years from now in which they can make profits, not only today. The same with the FDA. The pharmaceutical corporations came out against dismantling the Food and Drug Administration. They'd maybe like it cut back, but they don't want to dismantle it. They are smart enough to figure out that if there is no regulation and independent assessment, five years from now there will be some kind of thalidomide catastrophe or something like that, and they'll lose their international markets. And so it goes. There has always been a symbiotic relationship between big private capital and state power. They want to maintain it.

If you look back over American business history, there is one rather systematic split. Tom Ferguson has done some very interesting work on that, as have others. There's been a consistent, pretty general distinction between capital-intensive, high-technology, internationally-oriented financial and industrial sectors on the one hand, which are the real big guys, and the labor-intensive, more domestically-oriented, less advanced technological parts of the system on the other. That's what's called "small business" here, but it's not small by any means. That difference shows up in all sorts of things. So you find it in the lobbying system, the Business Council and more recently the Business Roundtable. That represents the big guys. They want a strong government. A lot of them in various forms even support New Deal measures. They instituted some of the New Deal measures. They were in favor of what they sometimes call welfare capitalism. They don't mean by that money that goes into their pockets. What they mean is keeping a decent life for the working class, benefits for your workers. Which doesn't cost them a lot. They are capital-intensive, not labor-intensive. They understand the point of a smoothly functioning society.

On the other hand, take the Chambers of Commerce, the National Association of Manufacturers, who typically represented the other sector. They have quite different policies on many issues. One of the things that's happening in Washington right now is an unusual shift of power toward the so-called small business side. The big business people are perfectly happy about it, as long as it keeps enriching them, which it's doing. But they're looking at it with a wary eye. The Gingrich Republicans talk a kind of populist line. They even talk an anti-corporate line. Of course, they do nothing about it. If they ever start doing something about it, it will be interesting to watch the hammer fall. I don't think they're going to last very long. As long as they talk their populist line but pour money into the pockets of the rich, they can talk their line if they like. But when a conflict really develops, I think they will be quietly sent on their way.

DB *You've always commented that you weren't too concerned if these guys—like let's take these Republican shock troops, as they're called, were the standard type of politician, skimming off the top, corrupt, etc.—that you would be concerned if they were different. Do you think they are different?*

I think they represent something different which is interesting and important. They represent a kind of proto-fascism. And that's dangerous. First of all, there's the religious fanaticism, which is a very dangerous thing. There's a cultural tone about them, which shows up all over the place, which has a very fascist character to it. All the things we've discussed reflect this. And there's a real sadism. They really want to go for the jugular. Anybody who doesn't meet their standards, which means, Enrich myself tomorrow, anybody who doesn't meet that condition, they just want to kill, not just oppose, but destroy. They are quite willing—cynics like Gingrich are extreme, but others are willing—to try to engender fear and hatred against immigrants and poor people. They are very happy to do that. Their attitudes are extremely vicious.

You can see it all over. Take the state of Alabama that has not only restored chain gangs, but chain gangs where they truck rocks in for people to smash up. That's real sadism. Also our governor, William Weld, who's supposed to be a moderate. He's one of the moderate Republicans, a nice guy type. Just last week every day in the newspapers there was another headline about forcing people out of homeless shelters if he didn't like the way they lived. Like some mother took off a day to take care of a mentally retarded child. Okay, out of the homeless shelter. He doesn't like that. He thinks she should work, not take care of her child. Some disabled veteran didn't want to move into a well-known drug den. Okay, out on the street. That's one day. Next day comes state welfare, social services, have to report to the INS if they think somebody may be an illegal immigrant. Then they get deported. Which means their child gets deported. Their child could well be an American citizen. So American citizens have to be deported, according to the governor, if he doesn't like the fact of the way their parents are here.

The real point of it, and his purpose, is to ensure that these children will starve to death because it means their parents won't be able to go to get services. They won't be able to go to school. So really kick the kids in the face. That's the idea. It goes on like this, day after day. It was a series of these through the week, like written by Jonathan Swift. One day was a headline about how he was giving I forget how much money, but a couple of million dollars, to the guys who were running racetracks. They were also cutting down a tiny little pittance that went to try to deal with compulsive gambling. Compulsive gambling is an addiction, as harmful as other addictions. But you want to increase that addiction, and there's a good reason for that. Gambling is a tax on the poor. His friends don't go to the racetracks. It's poor people who go to the racetracks, just like poor people buy lottery tickets. His friends don't. That's just another one of those massively regressive taxes on the poor. So let's increase that and furthermore put more state funds into the hands of the racetrack owners who are doing it.

This is day after day. Pure sadism. Very self-conscious. He's not a fool. And he's trying to build public support for it by building up fear and hatred. The idea is, There's these teenage kids (who are black, by implication, although you don't say that in a liberal state) who are just ripping us off by having lots and lots of babies. We don't want to let them do that. So let's hate them and let's kick them in the face while I'm kicking you in the face. That's real fascism. And that's the liberal side. It's not the Gingrich shock troops. That's the liberal, moderate, educated side.

This runs across the spectrum. Take a look at it. This combination of extreme religious fanaticism, hysteria, intolerance, viciousness, sadism, fear, hatred, but with people who understand it very well, like Newt Gingrich, William Weld, and others, is a technique to ensure the increase of totalitarian power in the hands primarily of the private tyrannies, which they work for, but also in the hands of an increasingly powerful state which is more and more dedicated to security systems and devices for transferring funds towards the wealthy. That's a prescription for fascism. That's dangerous.

DB *You said the economic system is a "grotesque catastrophe." What kind of system would you propose?*

That's the topic for another discussion. I would propose a system which is democratic. It's long been understood (this has nothing to do with the left per se; it's right through the American working-class movement, and independent social thinkers) that you don't have democracy unless people are in control of the major decisions. And the major decisions, as has also long been understood, are fundamentally investment decisions: What do you do with the money? What happens in the country? What's produced? How is it produced? What are working conditions like? Where does it go? How is it distributed? Where is it sold? That whole range of decisions, that's not everything in the world, but unless that range of decisions is under democratic control, you have one or another form of tyranny. That is as old as the hills and as American as apple pie. You don't have to go to Marxism or anything else. It's straight out of mainstream American tradition.

The reason is simple common sense. So that's got to be the core of it. That means total dismantling of all the totalitarian systems. The corporations are just as totalitarian as Bolshevism and fascism. They come out of the same intellectual roots, in the early twentieth century. So just like other forms of totalitarianism have to go, private tyrannies have to go. And they have to be put under public control.

Then you look at the modalities of public control. Should it be workers' councils or community organizations or some integration of them? What kind of federal structure should there be? At this point you're beginning to think about how a free and democratic society might look and operate. That's worth a lot of thought. But we're a long way from that. The first thing you've got to do in any kind of change is to recognize the forms of oppression that exist. If slaves don't recognize that slavery is oppression, it doesn't make much sense to ask them why they don't live in a free society. They think they do. This is not a joke.

Take women. Overwhelmingly, and for a long time, they may

have sensed oppression, but they didn't see it as oppression. They saw it as life. The fact that you don't see it as oppression doesn't mean that you don't know it at some level. At some level you know it. The way in which you know it can take very harmful forms for yourself and everyone else. That's true of every system of oppression. But unless you sense it, identify it, understand it, understand furthermore that it's not, as in that *New Yorker* article, the genius of the market and a mystery, but completely understandable and not a genius of anything, and easily put under popular control—unless all those things are understood, you cannot proceed to the next step, which is the one you raised: How can we change the system?

I think you can figure out how to change the system by reading the independent working class press 150 years ago that we talked about earlier. These were ordinary working people, artisans, "factory girls" from New England farms, and so on. They knew how to change the system. You know, too. They were strongly opposed to what they called "the New Spirit of the Age: Gain wealth, forgetting all but Self." They wanted to retain the high culture they already had, the solidarity, the sympathy, the control. They didn't want to be slaves. They thought that the Civil War was fought to end slavery, not to institute it. All of these things are perfectly common perceptions, perfectly correct. You can turn them into ways in which a much more free society can function.

Israel

Rewarding the Cop on the Beat

January 6, 1996

DB *The French government is trying to impose its own version of class warfare on French workers. The response has been rather dramatic. There have been wide-scale demonstrations, effectively shutting down the country. What do you think of that?*

It's really not anything particularly special that the French government is doing. It's applying a version of neoliberal structural adjustment, which is rammed down the throats of the Third World. They have no choice. It's increasingly being applied in the industrial societies as well, the U.S. and Britain considerably in the lead, but in a globalized economy others are being dragged along in one way or another. The difference in France was primarily the response, not the programs. There remains a tradition of working-class solidarity and activism that surprised a lot of people, and that's what happened. I don't think it will basically have an effect. The manifestation of it was interesting and important and could be one of the many strands initiating other comparable reactions, which could have a mutually reinforcing character sooner or later.

DB *Were you surprised?*

Yes. It hasn't happened in other places where people have been hit much harder.

DB *Strikingly, it didn't happen in Decatur, Illinois, where just about at the same time this thing was going on in France the eighteen-month UAW strike at Caterpillar just collapsed.*

It did collapse, you're right. But it was interesting to see how. Most of the work force voted against capitulating. The contract was a complete capitulation to Caterpillar. That's recognized on all sides. It was a "rout," as the business press called it. The workers at the plant voted 80% against it. The union leadership decided to accept it, and may have been right. Their point is that the forces were so unequal that the chances of their holding out were very slim. But it's not comparable to France. There it was a matter of working-class solidarity. But working-class solidarity is actually illegal in the U.S. We don't have things like general strikes or even secondary boycotts. They're excluded by law. The laws are designed to undermine the possibility of acting on general class interests or other general interests, which is quite unusual among industrial societies. Maybe unique, at least among the more democratic ones.

In France this was a national issue. Hardly anyone here knew about the Decatur situation. There was barely any coverage of anything that had been happening, except in the business press now and then or, let's say, the *Chicago Tribune*, the kind of papers that are business-oriented and nearby. But very few people knew anything about it. As you recall, when Decatur workers came to the Boston area to try to raise some support, they could barely get any people out to a meeting, which is very unusual. Almost anything gets a big crowd under comparable circumstances. So they were left alone, hanging on a limb.

Caterpillar was in an extremely strong position. Like corporate America generally, it has made huge profits in recent years. It had, I think, about 40% or 50% profit growth in the last year. And they've used their profits for a very sensible business strategy. These are people who are fighting a bitter class war. They've used them to create excess capacity overseas so that, as they explain to the business press, they could undermine any workers' actions by simply using their other facilities, many overseas, to ensure that they maintain their market. Also, in the U.S., again unusual, maybe unique among industrial societies, it's permitted to employ permanent replacement workers, which is worse than scabs, to destroy strikes. The U.S. has been cited for that by the International Labor Organization, but it continues. And a huge number of part-time workers, and so on. So Caterpillar was in a very strong position to carry out a very efficient class war in a successful effort to undermine some of the last remnants of American unionism.

There was very little general solidarity, in part because there was simply no awareness. The thing was kept under wraps. Also because the options for common action have been very much undercut, in part simply by legal measures and in part by a huge onslaught of propaganda to just simply drive such ideas out of people's minds and leave them alone, facing awesome power by themselves.

DB *One other thing about the Caterpillar strike in Decatur: There have been almost Stalinist-like restrictions on the returning workers.*

Not "almost." The *Wall Street Journal* had an article which was headlined by saying that workers have gag rules imposed. The company will allow some workers to return, which is already pretty outlandish, but they are under a gag rule which requires that they say nothing about the strike. They say nothing critical of management. They don't wear T-shirts that have something that the company considers harmful to its reputation. It's straight Stalinist. It's not "Stalinist-like."

DB *Let's move on that note of Stalin to Russia. Recent elections there indicate a revival of support for the Communist Party. Is that entirely unexpected?*

I don't quite interpret it that way. It's not just in Russia. It's all over Eastern Europe. The standard version, which is actually given in a *New York Times* report that I'm almost quoting, is that nostalgia for the past is increasing as it recedes further into the distance. I don't think there's any indication of nostalgia for the Stalinist dungeon. It's not that the past is receding. It's that the present is approaching, and the present happens to be Brazil and Mexico. However horrifying the Soviet socioeconomic system might have been, the way people live in the comparable countries that we run are, for the most part, much worse. So for the large majority of the population of places like, say, Brazil, Guatemala, or Mexico, the conditions of Eastern Europe would have seemed very impressive indeed. Now what the people of Eastern Europe are seeing is that they are being returned to Third World conditions, the conditions of countries that we've been running for a long, long time. And as that approaches, they don't like it. Just as if the population in our own domains had a choice, they wouldn't like it, either. And that's what I think one is seeing, not a kind of revival of love for the dungeon that has disappeared.

DB *Moving on to Haiti, there were elections there also very recently. Generally, U.S. commentary has been very critical of Jean-Bertrand*

Aristide and the Lavalas movement.

It's actually mixed. First of all, it's important to recognize that certain critical facts are still kept very, very quiet. One is that there was no embargo, to speak of. To mention one striking example, public but still largely supressed, the Bush and Clinton administrations authorized Texaco to ship oil illegally to the junta and its rich supporters. The second is that Aristide was allowed to return under very strict conditions, an extreme form of structural adjustment, exactly what the public voted *against* in the 1990 election that so scandalized U.S. power. He hasn't entirely been living up to them. Haiti is in a way like France. It's one of the few countries where there has been popular resistance to the imposition of these neoliberal structural adjustment programs. Aristide has roots among the people, and he has to some extent reflected that and has not gone along as willingly as have the usual Third World elites with the orders from Washington, the World Bank, and the IMF. Haiti has been punished for that. The very limited funds that have been offered have indeed been withheld because of their refusal to undergo a program which would essentially dismantle the entire governmental system and turn it over to private power to an unprecedented extent. They've been dragging their feet on that. There's been a lot of popular resistance. As a result, Aristide is criticized.

But the democratic structures which swept him into power, the grassroots movements, have not been demolished by years of terror. And although he has—lacking any alternative, in my opinion—gone along pretty much with the external power that allowed him to return, he hasn't done it with the proper willingness and enthusiasm and devotion to the masters, which does arouse criticism.

DB *Do you know anything about the new president, René Préval?*

He's been close to Aristide and does reflect pretty much the same views. I think he has essentially the same base of support.

DB *Haiti was an example of what is called "humanitarian intervention." Somalia is another. Bosnia is also cited. Are there instances where you would support such actions?*

First of all, I suppose just about every military action in history has been described as humanitarian intervention. They may not have used that term, but some similar one. It's always with very noble purposes. And if you try to find genuine examples in history of authentic humanitarian intervention, you're going to find pretty slim pickings. On the other hand, I don't think you can give a general principle about when the use of military force is legitimate. It depends on what the alternatives are. So there are circumstances in which maybe that's the least bad of the available alternatives. You just have to look at things on a case-by-case basis. There are some general principles that one can adhere to, but they don't lead to specific conclusions for every conceivable case.

DB *I know on Bosnia you received many requests for support of intervention to stop what people called "genocide." Was it genocide?*

"Genocide" is a term that I myself don't use even in cases where it might well be appropriate.

DB *Why not?*

I just think the term is way overused. Hitler carried out genocide. That's true. It was in the case of the Nazis a determined and explicit effort to essentially wipe out populations that they wanted to disappear from the face of the earth. That's genocide. The Jews and the Gypsies were the primary victims. There were other cases where there has been mass killing. The highest per capita death rate in the world since the 1970s has been East Timor. In the late 1970s it was by far in the lead. Nevertheless, I wouldn't call it genocide. I don't think it was a planned effort to wipe out the entire population, though it may well have killed off a quarter or so of the population. In the case of Bosnia—where the proportions killed are far less—it was horrifying, but it was certainly far less than that, whatever judgment one makes, even the more extreme judgments. I just am reluctant to use the term. I don't think it's an appropriate one. So I don't use it myself. But if people want to use it, fine. It's like most of the other terms of political discourse. It has whatever meaning you decide to give it. So the question is basically unanswerable. It depends what your criteria are for calling something genocide.

On the calls for military intervention, they were of an interesting character. They were very vague. I've never seen, during all these years in which there's been a lot of laments about the collapse of Western civilization and so on, I just didn't see any substantive proposals as to what could be done. Do something, was what people said. Send troops. But what are they going to do? The substantive proposals were extremely slim. What has been done I think is quite ugly. What has been done, and I think this has been in the works for a long time, is essentially leading to an effective partition of the region, the former Yugoslavia. Slovenia is out of it, but except for that, the rest of it into a Greater Serbia and Greater Croatia, with Bosnia pretty much partitioned. They may call it a state, but part of it will be part of Croatia and part of it will be part of Serbia.

Greater Croatia is already pretty much a U.S. client. The U.S. has been helping it arm and has been supporting it. And I think that the U.S. anticipates the same will be true of Greater Serbia, so if it works out that way it will place the U.S. in effective control of the former Yugoslavia, which is pretty much a return to the previous status quo. That region has considerable significance. From the U.S. perspective it's always been regarded as part of the periphery of the Middle East, the whole system of protection and control over energy resources.

It's also a kind of a base for entry into the restored Third World of Eastern Europe, where there are common interests among the major industrial powers, but there are also conflicts. So the U.S. has somewhat different ideas about how to exploit Eastern Europe from those of, say, France and Germany. The base in the Balkans places the U.S. in a position to implement its own power interests and economic interests. So a U.S. takeover of that region, or, more accurately, a retakeover of the region, is not an unexpected goal of foreign policy. What the U.S. has done is sort of stand on the sidelines as long as it was tough going there. When it looked as if a military balance had been established, primarily by U.S. aid to Croatia and indirect aid to the Bosnian Muslims—which in fact the U.S. actually let Iran do a lot of—now that that balance was more or less set and it looked as though it would be possible simply to insert U.S. forces to separate warring armies without too much threat or danger, and of course commitment to use massive force if anything goes wrong, then the U.S. sent in troops.

Now suppose I had been in Congress, let's say, and had been asked to choose between exactly two alternatives. One, let them keep massacring one another. Two, put in U.S. troops to separate warring armies, to partition the country into two U.S. dependencies with a possibility that something may go badly wrong, as in Somalia, and there might be a huge slaughter. If those are the two choices, I probably would have voted for sending the troops.

DB *What about Germany's interests in and links to Croatia? Do you think that's significant?*

It's very significant. Germany took the initiative in the early stages, in a very premature recognition of Slovenia and Croatia and Bosnia-Herzgovina. Slovenia was sort of reasonable, I suppose. But in the case of Croatia and Bosnia-Herzgovina, the recognition was first a German initiative, and the European Union went along very quickly, without any concern for a rather serious question, namely, the rights of substantial Serbian minorities. That's not to justify the way they reacted, but there were legitimate concerns and they were not taken into account. That was just a prescription for disaster.

DB *Misha Glenny and others have cited the German recognition as igniting Serb fears of a resurgence of German power in the Balkans. They have memories there.*

They have plenty of memories. Everybody has memories. Again, none of this is justification for what happened. But the recognition of the independence of Croatia and Bosnia-Herzgovina without any concern for this obviously quite serious problem was throwing a match into a can of gasoline.

DB *It seems to me that Clinton was very anxious to supplant U.N. forces with NATO. Do you agree?*

Only at the right moment. As long as it was difficult, they wanted U.N. forces in there. As long as there was fighting and danger and difficulties in getting humanitarian supplies, the U.S. wanted to be out of it. NATO means the U.S. It's a cover for the U.S. The U.S. only wants to move in when the game is over and it can pick up the pieces. So the hard work was done by the Europeans. You can ask how well they did it. Pretty badly, I think. But nevertheless, it was their task. The U.S. was on the sidelines. It was willing to bomb but nothing else. By the time it seemed as if the conflict had a possible resolution by insertion of force, massive force, that would not be under any threat, by the time that looked possible, the Clinton administration wanted the U.N. out and wanted to take over. It's not very different from Somalia. In the case of Somalia, as long as the conflict was raging and there was a terrible famine and people were dying and there were a lot of murders, the U.S. just simply stayed out, didn't want anything tô do with it. When the fighting was declining and it looked like there was going to be a good harvest and there was a fair chance that the famine was ending, the Red Cross and other efficient agencies were getting food through—at that point the U.S. moved in with a massive show of force and a huge PR operation, expecting to get a lot of at least favorable publicity out of it. Indeed, that would have happened if it hadn't been for U.S. military doctrine, which is unusual. It requires that U.S. forces never be put under any threat at all. If someone looks at them the wrong way, we call out the helicopter gunships. That's why the U.S. is pretty much disqualified from peacekeeping operations that involve civilians. And they've made it very clear, incidentally, in Bosnia, that they're going to do the same thing. Massive force if anybody gets in their way, unlike these wishy-washy Europeans, who don't just kill anybody in sight. In Somalia it led to a disaster. According to U.S. sources, somewhere between 7500 and 10,000 Somali civilians were killed before the U.S. forces were withdrawn. And that was not a very conflictive situation.

DB *You're saying that the U.S. was responsible directly for those deaths?*

A good bit of it. Just violent overreaction to minor provocations, the kind of thing that other countries don't respond to. For example, at the same time that U.S. forces went into Bosnia, with huge coverage and front-page stories, if you really looked into the back pages and the small items, you might discover that at that very same time, Norwegian peacekeeping forces in Southern Lebanon were attacked by Israeli tanks and several were severely wounded and hospitalized. We don't have the rest of the story because it wasn't reported. If anything like that happened to U.S. forces, even anything far less than that, there would have been a massive military response.

DB *Can't also the U.S. point to these kinds of interventions as a justification for continued massive military spending?*

Sure. It's used for that, in fact. The Somali intervention was pretty openly described that way. Colin Powell and others put it in pretty much those terms, pointing out that the Pentagon budget was in trouble and they needed some good public relations.

DB *Let's turn now to focus on the Middle East. It is received wisdom that the September 1995 Oslo accord has pretty much settled the Israeli-Palestinian question. Typical headlines were, "Israel Agrees to Quit West Bank." "At the White House, Symbols of a Day of Awe." "The Undeniable Reality: The Palestinians are on Their Way to an Independent State; the Jews are Bidding Farewell to Portions of the Holy Land to which They Have Historically Felt Most Linked," and on and on. You take exception to those views.*

Not entirely. I think some of it is correct. It is a day of awe. It was a tremendous victory for the rule of force in international affairs, a very impressive one, and a extraordinary doctrinal victory as well. Maybe that should inspire awe. It's possible that it may resolve the conflict pretty much the way that the great powers have been doing in Bosnia may resolve that conflict by partitioning it. There are ways to resolve things. The problem of the Native Americans was resolved. They're not around any more. So the problem was resolved. The Israel-Palestine problem may be resolved in the same fashion. Certainly the Oslo agreements are a long step towards it.

On the other hand, the factual descriptions are just farcical. Israel didn't quit the West Bank. It indicated no intention of quitting the West Bank. In fact, it made very clear its intention, and its intention means Washington's intention, because otherwise it doesn't happen. So Washington made clear with its Israeli client that it would not quit the West Bank. On and on the rest of the story is just the most outlandish fabrication. Just simply look at the bare facts. This agreement didn't deal with the Gaza Strip, where Israel retains the roughly 30% it wanted. And in fact in its recent budget it has just assigned that part of the Gaza Strip to Israel itself. It places it under the budget for the Negev. That cuts off the areas assigned to Palestinian administration from any access to the Arab world.

In the West Bank, which was covered by the Oslo agreement of September 28, they divided it into four areas. One area is total Israeli control. That's 70%. Another area is given to Palestinian administration, the municipal areas of a half-dozen cities. That's 2%. The remainder, roughly 28%, consists of about a hundred isolated sectors within the Israeli 70% which are given local autonomy under overall Israeli control. There's a fourth region, that's Jerusalem, which Israel has already annexed. Jerusalem means Greater Jerusalem, a big, expanding area, a substantial part of the West Bank. It's kind of intriguing that if you look at the maps, not only in Israel but in the *New York Times*, they simply assign that area to Israel. So the *New York Times* map colors it the same color as Israel. The West Bank is everything but that. So that region, though theoretically up for negotiation, has already been assigned to Israel by itself and the U.S. government and the *New York Times*. So those are the four areas. To talk about Israel withdrawing from the West Bank under those conditions is ridiculous. It becomes even more absurd when you look at the further conditions.

Israel retains veto power over any legislation passed by Palestinians anywhere in any of the areas where they have a degree of local autonomy. The Palestinian authorities are required, and agreed, to accept the legality of Israeli rights in the West Bank and Israeli sovereignty over what Israel will determine to be state lands or absentee lands. Those are pretty loose categories, but they will amount to essentially what Israel feels like keeping. That, incidentally, totally undermines U.N. 242, completely dismantles it, the basic diplomatic framework, which called for withdrawal from the territories. And it completely rescinds the decisions of the Security Council and of just about every government in the world that the settlements are illegal and that Israel has no sovereign rights in the territories. That's all rescinded. The Palestinian Authority agrees to accept that Israel does have sovereign rights there and what it does is legal and legitimate.

There was great talk about the amazing transformation in Yitzhak Rabin. He was willing to concede. Israel was willing to make a "historic compromise." Simply compare what they took in Oslo II with what they had been calling for at the peak period of refusal to have any dealings whatsoever with the Palestinians or to recognize any of their rights. So in 1988, for example, when the U.S. and Israel were refusing any dealings with the Palestinians, any recognition of

Palestinian rights, an extreme point of rejectionism, at that point Yitzhak Rabin was Defense Minister, and he called for keeping 40% of the West Bank and Gaza. They didn't want the rest. That's the traditional position. Now they've got between 70% and 98%, depending on how you estimate it. About twice as much as what they had asked for at their most extreme position.

I don't think they're going to keep that much. It would be crazy. In subsequent imposed agreements, I presume that they'll reduce their own integration of the territories to what they've always wanted.

Meanwhile, it's not just words. It's also actions on the ground. So the new budget, which was just passed by the Knesset, the Parliament, in late November, after Oslo II and after the Rabin assassination, calls for tens of millions of dollars for new settlements in the West Bank, the Gaza Strip, and the Golan Heights, funded as usual by the American taxpayer in one or another fashion. It offers even inducements for new settlers. This includes, just to show how extreme it is: There are new settlers who go to the Gaza Strip, which is a very arid area where people don't have drinking water. They will be given special subsidies for fish ponds in the new budget. That's typical. Meanwhile, Israel's military budget is going up, but mostly for the construction of what they call "bypass roads," a big network of infrastructure roads that will enable Jewish settlers on the West Bank to travel freely without even seeing scattered Arab villages which are isolated from one another and will disappear somehow. It also cantonizes the region, breaks it into separate areas. So whatever local autonomy is granted won't have any larger significance.

DB *In a Z magazine article you make an analogy with the Oslo accords and New York State ceding authority over certain areas. What was that?*

It's kind of as if the New York State authorities decided to cede control of the South Bronx and the slums of Buffalo to local authorities, meanwhile taking the wealthy urban areas, the useful land, the resources, the commercial and financial centers, in fact, anything they wanted. They'd be delighted to do that if they could.

DB *How do the Oslo accords treat the question of Palestinian refugees, right of return, and/or compensation?*

That's simply gone. There's nothing there for the refugees. Yitzhak Rabin and his colleagues have made it very clear and explicit that they are not going to get anything. They're out of the game. The U.S. backs that. Remember, everything that happens there happens because the U.S. backs it. Otherwise it does not happen. So this is U.S. policy, much more extreme under Clinton than his predecessors, incidentally. The idea is to somehow just scatter them like human waste sômewhere. That is in direct violation of long-standing international agreements going right back to the U.N. Declaration of Human Rights in December 1948, one provision of which called for the right of return of people to territories from which they had been expelled. The explicit intention was to affirm the Palestinians' right. This was made clear and explicit the next day, when the U.N. unanimously, including the U.S., endorsed the right of Palestinians specifically to return or compensation under this provision, Article 13 of the U.N. Declaration of Human Rights. That's all gone. It's never been more than rhetoric, but now even the rhetoric's gone.

DB *Are you saying that Washington runs everything and there's no such thing as Israeli sovereignty?*

Oh, no. It's not that there's no such thing as Israeli sovereignty. The state of Nevada has some sovereignty, too. But Washington's influence is overwhelming. Remember, Israel gets a degree of foreign support that is just off the scale. There's no country that even comes close. You can't call it the fifty-first state of the Union, because no state gets anywhere near that amount of per capita aid from the federal government. There's no country in the world that compares. It's just not on the spectrum. U.S. influence in the region is overwhelming. The U.S. controls the major oil producers. Egypt's a client. Turkey is pretty much a client. Pakistan often has been. As long as the Shah was in power, Iran was another client. Of course, control is not total. It's not even total in Central America. But it's very extensive. In the case of Israel, the dependency is extremely high.

DB *In that same Z article, you say that the U.S. gives $3 billion annually to Israel, "perhaps twice that if we add other devices." What are those devices, and how does Israel command that level of U.S. aid?*

There's a whole range of devices which have been looked into in some detail by people like Donald Neff and others, who have arrived at the $6 billion figure. They include loans that are turned into grants, delaying payment, all sorts of financial trickery, handover of technology. There's a whole mass of devices. I think that Neff's rough estimate of about $6 billion probably isn't too far from the mark. The $3 billion alone is unprecedented. How does Israel get that degree of aid? There's debate over that. There have basically been two positions. This is independent of whether you support or oppose it. People, whatever position they take on that, have divided over two factors. One is the domestic lobby. The second is the strategic role that Israel plays in U.S. general global policy. My own view is that it's the second factor that's largely responsible for this.

DB *The one you called the "local cop on the beat"?*

It's not I who called it that. I'm borrowing the term from Richard Nixon's Secretary of Defense.

DB *Melvin Laird. While police headquarters remain in Washington.*

That's my term. So his words were, "We need local cops on the beat." I just added a little gloss: And police headquarters remain in Washington.

DB *Whether it's the $3 billion official figure or the $6 billion one, that's an awfully high salary to pay for a cop.*

The U.S. gets a lot out of it. Take that $3 billion. A lot of it is military aid. What's military aid? Military aid is payment by the U.S. taxpayer to U.S. corporations. That's money that doesn't move out of U.S. banks. Incidentally, that's true of a lot of foreign aid. You want to maintain the high-tech sector of the U.S. economy. The way we do that is under a military cover. One way of doing it is producing and exporting high-technology waste. That's the majority of the $3 billion.

Then there's plenty more that's involved. There are mutual operations in technology development. There's intelligence sharing. Israel has been a mercenary state. For example, when Congress imposed human rights constraints on the Carter and Reagan administrations and wouldn't let them participate directly in the ongoing slaughters in Guatemala, they could turn to Israel for help. Not just Israel, also Taiwan, Britain, Argentine neo-Nazis. The U.S. is a big boy on the block. It has big terror networks. But Israel has been a big part of this in Africa, Latin America, Asia, and elsewhere. But its primary role is as a crucial part of the system of support of the family dictatorships that the British used to call the "Arab façade" that manages the energy resources and ensures that the profits flow to the West. There has always been a kind of tacit alliance between Israel and Saudi Arabia. And now it's likely to come more to the surface. That's an important role. In fact, if you take a look at U.S. aid, it shot up in 1967, after Israel smashed the Egyptian forces of Nasser, which were the leading forces for independence in the Arab world and considered a great danger. Israel smashed that. Aid to Israel shot up.

It went up again, in fact more than quadrupled, in 1970, when Jordan was carrying out a massacre of Palestinians. It looked for a moment as though Syria might intervene to support the Palestinians, at which point the U.S. asked Israel to just mobilize to bar that, and it did. "Black September," as it was called, could continue. That was considered very important. Henry Kissinger himself described it as one of the most important contributions that Israel made, and military aid shot up. So it continues. These are some of the reasons why I'm skeptical about the domestic lobbying interpretation. In my view domestic lobbies work insofar as they line up with major power interests. Then they may have an effect, even a swing effect. But not an independent effect.

DB *Is there a figure on how much money the U.S. has given to Israel since 1948? Does anybody know?*

Sure, you can find it out. It wasn't enormous, it wasn't high until 1967. Virtually all Israeli capital formation up till 1967 was from external sources, either from the U.S. or German reparations. Remember that the U.S. gives aid in another way, too. Israel is the only country to which it is possible to make tax-free donations. If you want to make tax-free donations for the purchase of land from which Arabs are excluded, you can do that tax-free in the U.S. And that amounts to a lot of money. So if you add up all the money, even up to 1967, it was pretty substantial. But after that it goes off the chart. In 1978, Israel was receiving more than half of official U.S. aid worldwide. It usually runs about a third. And that's just official aid. It doesn't count the other stuff.

DB *It's been suggested already that if there is a Syria-Israel deal on the Golan Heights that the U.S. will essentially pay the bill.*

In a sense it will pay the bill, but the U.S. pays the bill for maintaining the state altogether to a large extent. Similarly with Egypt. Take a look at U.S. foreign aid. The biggest component of it is Israel, Egypt, and Turkey. It has included Pakistan. It varies a bit over the years, so there have been years when El Salvador was up there. But over a long period it's basically those states. Per capita, of course, that means overwhelmingly Israel. That's all part of the system of what the Nixon administration called the "local cops on the beat." The Arab façade ensures that the flow of profits from oil go to the West, mainly to the U.S. and Britain, and not to the people of the region. That Arab façade needs protection from its own population. There has always been a ring of gendarmes that provides that protection, and they get supported.

DB *The* New York Times *is writing articles saying, Tel Aviv is "awash" with luxury cars. Israel is a "rich" country. Its standard of living is higher than a couple of European states.*

It's a rich country thanks largely to outside aid. On the other hand, remember it's a U.S. client, which means it's coming to resemble the U.S. So it has a very high proportion of the population living in poverty, and it has extremely high inequality. I think it's second only to the U.S. among the rich countries.

DB *But the question arises, in this time of so much obsession with fiscal austerity and budget cuts, why is this money not being a topic of debate?*

How about the subsidies to the wealthy in the U.S.? Is that a topic of debate? The Pentagon budget just went up. Fiscal austerity means fiscal austerity for the poor, not for the rich. Here's some figures from Israel, if you're interested, from the *Jerusalem Post* a few weeks ago. Headline: "Record 670,000 Lived Under Poverty Line in 1994, an increase of about 24,000 over 1993." Going up very fast. As the wealth is going up. In this respect it's quite similar to the U.S.

But "fiscal austerity" is a term that is not intended seriously. There's no fiscal austerity for the Fortune 500, who have just celebrated their fourth straight year of double-digit profit growth. Part of the reason for that profit growth is precisely federal subsidy. These guys have forgotten what capitalism is even supposed to be. There was a front-page article in the *Wall Street Journal* the other day. Two states, Maryland and Virginia, were competing with different strategies for economic development. For a while, Maryland was going ahead, and then Virginia did. The article is all full of talk about their entrepreneurial values and business-friendly climate and what great success stories they are. Virginia is now in the lead. Take a look closely and you'll notice that it's not Virginia and Maryland. It's the parts of Virginia and Maryland that border on Washington. The difference of strategy that's being followed is that Maryland has been banking on biotechnology, expecting to rip off the National Institutes of Health, and Virginia has been banking on electronics and high tech, counting on ripping off the Pentagon budget. That's their business strategy: Which part of the federal government can we use to subsidize us? The reason why Virginia is doing better is that they picked the winner at the moment, namely, the Pentagon system, which is the traditional technique for maintaining high technology. That's called "entrepreneurial capitalism."

DB *That creates the "opportunity society" that the right wing touts.*

There's no fiscal austerity there. There's fiscal austerity for children whose mothers don't live the way Newt Gingrich says they should.

DB *Let's get back to the Middle East. In writing and speaking on the topic you sometimes cite Israel Shahak as a source. Who is he?*

Israel Shahak has been for many years Israel's leading civil libertarian. He's a militant civil libertarian who, since shortly after the 1967 war, has been defending Palestinian rights and the rights of other oppressed people, no matter who's oppressing them, whether it's the Palestinian authorities and the PLO or Israel. He also writes quite a lot about religious coercion and its effects, which are quite extreme in Israel, and on many other topics. He also is an invaluable source of information on any number of topics. He also circulates to people who read Hebrew tons of stuff from the Hebrew press. He does a lot of translations which have been very useful. The Israeli press covers things, for example, the occupied territories, with considerable accuracy, way beyond anything that one finds here. So he's been a very valuable source. He himself is a Holocaust survivor. He was a child in the Warsaw ghetto and ended up after the ghetto uprising in Bergen-Belsen for a couple of years and then went to Israel. We've been personal friends for many years.

DB *You've always been critical of Yasir Arafat and his leadership of the PLO. Have you seen anything in the last few months that would perhaps cause you to reassess your view?*

Yes. It's getting worse.

DB *In what way?*

I've always been critical, back to the time when he emerged in the late 1960s, pretty harshly critical all through, but now it's getting much worse. The repression in the West Bank is quite serious. It's reaching as far as even not just the usual targets, but very visible figures, leading human rights activists, editors, and so on. The control of the electoral process reached such a level of absurdity that it was condemned by European Union observers. Israel had made it very clear what kind of arrangement they were making with Arafat right after the first Oslo agreement. Yitzhak Rabin, who was Prime Minister (this is now September 1993, the "great breakthrough"), was explaining it to his party, the Israeli Labor Party, or maybe it was to the Parliament. He pointed out that it would be a good idea to have Arafat's forces carry out local administration, that is, run the local population, instead of the Israeli military, because then there won't be any complaints to the High Court or protests to human rights organizations or mothers and fathers and bleeding hearts. In other words, they can do a good job. Israel in fact is shifting to the traditional form of colonial control, at last. When the British ran India, or white South Africans and Rhodesians ran their countries, they tried not to use their own troops. They overwhelmingly used local mercenaries. The U.S. does the same in Central America. We try to use the security forces. If it's necessary, U.S. troops go in, but local mercenaries called state security forces or paramilitary forces are much more efficient, for exactly the reasons that Rabin said. That's the role that the Palestinian Authority is supposed to play. And if Arafat doesn't play it he's not going to last long. That's the deal he made with Israel. In return, they will be treated very well, like Third World elites generally.

DB *It's interesting to contrast U.S. aid to Israel and U.S. generosity to the Palestinians, for example. The U.S. is committed to providing $500 million over five years. That's 100 million bucks a year. It's not much money.*

It's virtually nothing. A couple of days ago I got a letter from an Israeli friend, a professor at Ben-Gurion University who runs the Israeli human rights group for Gaza. He travels there. He told me there's terrible poverty and this and that. There's some construction and development going on, and no sign of any U.S. money. What money there is is from the European Union or some other source.

DB *Early this morning I was looking at your 1974 book* Peace in the Middle East? *It had a question mark at the end. You were part of a group that had a vision of a binational state in Palestine. It seems that events have gone in a diametrically opposite direction. Is there any chance to revive that dream?*

Yes. In fact, I think that's the only plausible outcome at this point. I was always pretty skeptical, as you recall, both in that book and later, about the two-state settlement ideas that were being proposed. They were, in fact, the international consensus for quite a few years. It never seemed to me very reasonable. Maybe some kind of federal arrangement or something. But at this point, the issue of two states is dead. There is not going to be any meaningful Palestinian state. It's over. In fact, there will be no full Israeli withdrawal as required by the international diplomatic framework that the U.S. helped to craft, then completely undermined. That's pretty clear. What is being instituted is a kind of an apartheid system, as has been pointed out by Israeli commentators, meaning something like the system that South Africa imposed in the 1950s, even with Bantustans, which they'll call maybe a Palestinian state. The right end result of that is to overcome apartheid, as in South Africa, and move to some sort of cantonal arrangement or federal arrangement or other form of arrangement that will recognize, ultimately (I hope not too far in the future), the equal rights of all people there, which is going to mean their communal rights as well.

DB *There never was much sympathy, as you look over this whole question over the last forty or fifty years, for the Palestinian side in the U.S. The little there was is virtually disappearing. For example, there was the Middle East Justice Network and its newsletter,* Breaking the Siege. *They're no longer in existence.*

You have to be a little cautious about that. The general American population has been in favor of a Palestinian state by about two to one for most of the time that polls were taken. And that's without hearing it anywhere. So as usual, there's a big difference between elite opinion and general opinion. But among elite circles you're absolutely right. So in the press and in elite discussion and journals of opinion, the Palestinians don't exist. They're just a bunch of terrorists. Just to give one trivial example: When the *New York Times* assigned Greater Jerusalem to Israel, did you hear a peep of protest?

DB *No, there was nothing. And also, the figure that is given for the settlers on the West Bank and Gaza always excludes Jerusalem. The figure in circulation is 130,000.*

Which is under half of the settlers. In fact, Teddy Kollek—who was the mayor of Jerusalem—is considered a great hero here, a great humanitarian and a marvelous person who was bringing about Arab-Israeli harmony in Jerusalem. What he was doing, in fact, was setting up highly discriminatory regulations and procedures to try to overcome the Arab majority in East Jerusalem, where the population was crammed into narrower and narrower quarters, not permitted to build while land was being confiscated and Jewish settlement was being heavily subsidized. He was very clear about it. He said, Look, I'm not going to do anything to help the Arabs unless it's needed for the benefit of Jews. He said, We'll improve their health standards because we don't want them to get cholera because maybe it'll spread to the Jewish population. But beyond that, nothing, except occasionally for some "picture-window effect," as he called it. That's what the U.S. taxpayer is funding. Not only that, but what American intellectuals are calling, as Irving Howe once put it, strides towards social democracy that are an inspiration to all of us.

DB *I know you're always kind of reluctant to suggest things for people to do. Might there be some avenues that people can pursue on this particular issue?*

Sure. This is one of the easiest ones there is.

DB *Why do you say that?*

There's a very well-established international consensus which the U.S. itself helped frame (in fact was instrumental in framing), which calls for total Israeli withdrawal from the occupied territories, period. That was the official U.S. position. The U.S. framed it. That could be reconstituted. It happened to collapse in the government under Kissinger's influence in 1971, but it's not an option because people aren't aware of it. Nor does there have to be any support whatsoever for aid policies that go toward carrying out what I just described in Jerusalem. What's called "aid" to Israel is a funny kind of aid. It's the kind of aid that's driving more and more people under the poverty line. It's aid in the usual sense: aid to some sectors, harming other sectors. That doesn't have to happen. Countries should receive aid. I don't think rich countries should have the priority for aid, but if they do, it doesn't have to be the kind that leads to a record number of people under the poverty line, going up higher than any rich country outside the U.S. It doesn't have to be that kind of aid any more than we have to have that social policy here. There's plenty that Americans can do, especially in this area, where the U.S. influence and power is so decisive. But of course, as usual, it requires first escaping from the tentacles of our propaganda system, which in this particular case is really awesome in its power.

DB *What's ahead for you? I know you have a trip coming up to India.*

I'm leaving in a couple of days.

DB *What are you going to be doing there?*

The usual thing. It's initially political talks organized by an

Institute of Economics in Delhi and extending around Delhi to Calcutta, Hyderabad, and Trivandrum. It's mostly political talks, some on linguistics and other topics.

DB *You were last in India twenty years ago?*

More than that. In 1972 I was there to give the Nehru Memorial Lectures.

DB *It will be interesting to talk to you about your impressions of India when you come back.*

I'm afraid when I look at my schedule my impressions are mostly going to be of airports and the insides of lecture halls.

DB *We started this series of interviews with you sort of contemplating winding down things at MIT and your teaching career there. Any further thoughts on that?*

No, not really. I have no definite plans. I forget what we talked about, that was a long time ago. It's very uncertain.

DB *But you want to keep your rigorous schedule of talks and incessant requests for interviews like this one at the current level?*

"Want" is a funny word for it.

DB *Is there much choice, with the level of demand?*

Not only that, but just a feeling that I'm not doing what I should.

DB *If you had your druthers, what would you rather be doing?*

It gets pretty wearing, but what I should be doing is way more of this kind of thing.

DB *Thanks a lot. Bon voyage!*

Index

R

S